THE HUNT FOR THE HIJACKED NERVE AGENT

A KD THORNE THRILLER

MICHAEL P. KING

Blurred Lines Press

The Hunt for the Hijacked Nerve Agent

Michael P. King

ISBN 978-1-952711-06-0

Cover design by Paramita Bhattacharjee at creativeparamita.com

"A thriller that offers an undeniably entertaining way to spend an afternoon at the beach."—*Kirkus Reviews*

Stolen nerve agent. Scheming terrorists. Federal agents running out of time.

A deadly nerve agent has been stolen from a federal containment facility. When the National Defense Agency is tasked with recovering it, operative KD Thorne and her partner Jeffery Blunt are put on point. Find the nerve agent. Eliminate the threat.

KD Thorne knows trouble. Four tours in Afghanistan, a stint at NASA that went sideways, a marriage gone bad. She needs to work to keep her head on straight.

But as she and Blunt track the nerve agent from pharma executives and a military contractor team through white supremacists to a European far right faction, her personal life comes unraveled.

Can KD and Blunt stop the terrorists and retrieve the nerve agent before it's released and innocents die?

The Hunt for the Hijacked Nerve Agent is a fast-moving thriller that will keep you turning pages. If you like pulse-pounding action and surprising plot twists, you'll love the first novel in the KD Thorne series.

For Sarah

1

A t 2:15 a.m., Major Howard Rawlings, Accelerated Results Associates, and three of his team—O'Malley, Toms, and Adler—crept across the hard-packed sand inside the razor wire perimeter of a level-four containment storage facility in the Arizona desert, staying in the shadows between the security lights. They all wore tactical gear, helmets, and facemasks. After they stopped in front of the fifth building, Rawlings whispered into his comms set. "How are we?"

Sebold, his fourth team member, was sitting in a utility van in the dark beyond the chain-link fence. He clicked through the video feeds on a tablet computer. "We still have control of the surveillance cameras. The patrol is on the far north side of the facility."

Rawlings turned to O'Malley. "Go."

O'Malley pushed a magnetic card connected to a phone-size tablet computer into the card reader on the door lock. A few seconds later, the bolt slid back. Adler handed a small black duffel to Rawlings, slid his AR-15 rifle off his shoulder, and stepped into the shadows beside the door to stand watch. Rawlings reached for the door handle.

"Are you sure this material is properly contained?" Toms asked.

Rawlings glanced over his shoulder. "It's inside a heavy-duty transportation canister. Completely safe."

Rawlings turned the door handle and pushed. The negative pressurization pulled air from around them into the room beyond. The lights came on automatically. The room was lined with shelves loaded with two-foot-long metal canisters. Rawlings, O'Malley, and Toms moved along the shelves, reading the numbers on the canisters.

"Here it is, Major," O'Malley said. He had his hand on a canister racked near the back wall.

Rawlings stepped up beside him and verified the numbers etched into the top. "Take it."

O'Malley shook out a Tyvek bag. He and Toms slid the canister off the shelf and zipped it into the bag.

In the meantime, Rawlings set the black duffel on the floor in the center of the room and unzipped it, revealing a stack of C-4 wired to an electronic detonator. He armed the detonator and pulled out its antenna. Then he spoke into his comms. "We're on our way."

"All clear," Sebold replied.

He nodded to O'Malley and Toms, who each picked up an end of the Tyvek bag. They scurried back across the yard, Adler guarding their rear as they made their way to a four-foot-high cut in the perimeter fence and disappeared into the dark. On a dirt track behind a rock outcropping, the utility van sat waiting. They put the Tyvek bag containing the canister into the back and climbed in. Then they pulled off their helmets and facemasks. Rawlings rubbed his crewcut head. "Anything on the monitor, Sebold?"

Sebold, sitting in the driver's seat, looked up from the tablet computer in his lap. "Patrol is back at command."

"Let's go."

As they drove away into the desert, Rawlings pulled a remote control from his jacket pocket and pressed the button. An explosion boomed from the storage building. He took out a burner phone and speed-dialed the one number in the address book. "We've got the nerve agent."

"Excellent."

He ended the call and pulled the phone chip. An hour later, he threw the phone and the chip out the window as they drove over a bridge across an arroyo.

FOUR DAYS LATER, in a honky-tonk on a rundown side street of a suburb of Washington, DC, Captain KD Thorne slipped off her barstool and walked out of the bar. She was tired of being ogled by the guys in the corner booth, and she needed to make an early start in the morning. She wasn't quite sure how she'd ended up in this dump. Lately, as the night wore on, she'd been finding herself in the kinds of bars she would never go to during daylight. She was a tall woman, handsome, not pretty, lean and hard-muscled, a thin scar on her left cheek a souvenir from a firefight during a long-ago deployment. She stumbled as she stepped through the doorway down onto the sidewalk. The night air felt moist, and the street noise seemed indistinct. She turned down the closest alley, her high heels clicking on the pavement, and the short skirt of her dress fluttering as she moved. She could feel at least two men following her, gaining ground over the last block, trying to move quietly until it would be too late for her to run. They were almost on her.

"Hey, sweetness," a voice said. "Where you going?"

She swung around, putting her hand on the wall as if she'd lost her balance. Her adrenaline kicked in, the fog rushing out of her mind. There were three men behind her now, young, athletic, all vaguely smiling as their eyes roamed over her. She was going to have to fight. She let her handbag drop to the pavement and slipped out of her high heels. "None of your business."

"How about if we help you?" the closest one said. He moved toward her.

"I don't need any help." She dropped into a boxer's crouch, put all her force into the first punch, and broke his nose.

He shuffled back, his hands on his face, blood running between his fingers. The other two rushed in, one grabbing her right arm while the other smacked her face. "We thought we'd be gentle, but I guess you want it rough."

He grabbed the front of her dress as he pushed her against the wall. She put a thumb in his eye. He lurched backward. She caught the side of his knee with her bare heel. There was a quiet snap, and he went down.

The guy who had her right arm pulled a knife from his pants pocket. She gripped his hand with both of hers, stepped into him, and turned his wrist. The knife scraped along his ribs before it fell from his hand. He scuttled back away from her.

She heard clapping from the end of the alley and turned. A big man was silhouetted by the streetlight behind him. She glanced quickly back over her shoulder. The three would-be rapists were gone. "What do you want?"

The man backed under the streetlight. About six feet, black, wearing khakis and a gray sports coat. "Slow your roll, Doc."

"Do I know you?"

"It's been a while. I've got to admit I wasn't sure you'd whip all three of them wearing that party dress."

"Sergeant Blunt."

"Not sergeant anymore. This what you do for entertainment these days?"

"Were you looking for me?"

"You presentable to sit in a diner?"

"Let me find my shoes and my bag."

They sat in a booth in an all-night diner across from a bus stop. Other than the two cops standing at the counter joking with the waitress, they were the only ones in the place.

Blunt smiled. "Don't think I've ever seen you in a dress before."

KD shrugged. "It's a new look."

The waitress, a young woman in cornrows, a mostly clean apron covering her tank top, came up to the booth. "What'll you have?"

Blunt glanced toward KD. "Coffee?"

She nodded.

"You need menus?"

"No, thank you."

She brought two mugs of coffee. "Sugar and creamer is on the table."

KD watched Blunt stir two sugars into his coffee. "You like it sweet."

"My coffee and my women."

"Bet your wife is the only one who still smiles when you say that." She sipped her coffee. "Why are we talking?"

"Heard you were looking for work, but now I think maybe you need an intervention."

"I've got everything under control."

"Uh-huh. Drunk and stupid. Rapists, okay, they deserve worse than a beating, but come on, Doc, is this what your life is going to be?"

"I haven't seen you in—what? Four or five years? Excuse me if I'm not feeling your concern." She drank some more coffee. "So what kind of work are you talking about? If you know I'm looking, you know I haven't been able to find a decent military posting."

"This is not really military. Well, it is and it isn't."

"It either is or it isn't."

"Look, I know you're in a bad patch. I'd be pissed off if I were you. Might even be doing some crazy shit. I ran into a little trouble myself awhile back, but I landed on my feet. Better than the teams. Pay's good, too. And none of the army BS."

"What do you do?"

"You need to talk to the boss about that."

"So it's some mercenary shit."

"No, ma'am. This is legit." He slid a cell phone across the table. "Clara Garcia. National Defense Agency. Give her a call. Take a meeting. What have you got to lose? You know who you are. You know you want to feel the rush, do something that matters." He tapped on the phone with his index finger. "Give her a call."

. . .

THE NEXT DAY, KD sat in her underwear at her laptop computer scanning through the offerings at the job fair for retired or recently separated military personnel. Community college teaching jobs, military contractor jobs, franchise business opportunities, military-related manufacturing jobs. This is what her job search had come down to. Slit my wrists, she thought.

She got up from the kitchen table in her furnished rental apartment and poured some more coffee. Then she walked back to the bedroom, made the bed—pulling the sheets tight and smoothing the comforter—and laid out her clothes for the day, black pantsuit, white shirt, black socks, black flats. She added simple gold hoop earrings and pulled her dark hair back in a loose ponytail. She looked in the mirror to put on some lipstick. All business. Time to go to the job fair.

In the morning she attended a lecture on translating military experience into the business language that recruiters would understand. She already knew everything that the speaker covered, but she had to go somewhere, and she couldn't bring herself to actually go to any walk-in interviews. She didn't want to leave the army, but she was beginning to think that coming up to DC to work her contacts in hopes of getting an army assignment was a waste of time. Everyone was telling her the same thing. No room at the inn. Deployments were ending. All the desk chairs had bodies sitting in them, and there was no need for a captain in the field, particularly one who'd been out of the game for four years on special assignment at NASA and had a blemish on her record. So here she was, looking for a day job she didn't want.

At lunchtime, she turned on her smartphone. No voice mail, no texts. She'd known Harry was a smooth-talking narcissist when she started sleeping with him. Known his wife was a hot wire. But she'd fallen right into it. The excitement of sneaking around. The rush of being wanted. The sex itself. Motels, closets, the back seats of cars. Whoever taught him to fuck had done the job right. She just hadn't thought that she'd be the one who'd get blamed if they got caught. He got a rap on the knuckles. She got shipped out "to protect his family." NASA assholes.

She had one last contact to check in with—a longshot to be sure —the colonel from her first assignment, retired now. How much had he really known about her, a fresh lieutenant making all the usual mistakes? Still, he might have a lead of some sort. She found Colonel Greenberg in the lobby of the Marriott, sitting in a chair next to a grouping of potted plants, reading something on his laptop computer. He looked the same, if older. A little fatter, a little balder, probably just as cranky as he'd always been.

"Colonel," she said.

He looked up. "Captain Thorne. Nobody calls me that anymore. Have a seat."

She sat on the end of the sofa cattycorner to him. "Thanks for meeting me."

He grunted and closed his computer. "I understand you want to stay in the army?"

"Yes sir. I need a posting. I don't care where."

"Let me speak frankly, Captain."

"Please do."

"I think you're a fine officer, but you've got two problems. First, you wrangled a special assignment at NASA, which tells everyone who matters that you don't want to be in the regular army. Second, you screwed that up with a personal matter. So now you realize how badly you want to be a soldier. You see how that looks?"

"Yes sir."

"I've called around on your behalf, talked to all my contacts, but I'm pretty much out of the loop these days. I haven't found anyone willing to take a chance on you. I'm sorry, that's just the way it is."

"So there's nothing—"

He shook his head. "I'm sorry."

"Thanks for trying. It means a lot."

"Good luck."

By four o'clock she wanted a drink so bad that she found herself standing on the street outside a bar without realizing how she'd gotten there. It looked dark and cool and familiar inside. But she knew if she had a drink this early, the rest of the day would be gone.

She stepped away from the door, took out her phone, and googled an after-work AA meeting.

Another church basement featuring church basement coffee and package cookies. Fifteen or eighteen people interspersed among folding chairs facing a man and a woman standing behind a table. Work clothes, business casual, a couple of jackets and ties. KD sat in the back by herself. She barely heard what anyone said. She chewed her cookie and sucked on her steaming coffee. She closed her eyes and breathed. She wasn't really an alcoholic. She was just bored. In pain and bored. If she could dig out of this ditch, find a posting, not drink during the day, she'd be all right.

After the meeting, she went back to her rental. When she went into the kitchen to get a Diet Coke, she noticed the cell phone Blunt had given her sitting on the kitchen counter by the refrigerator. If she went back to that job fair, she'd either end up at a bar or another AA meeting. Why not take a chance? Couldn't be worse than the jobs she'd been looking at. She speed-dialed the one number in the phone.

A woman's voice spoke. "Captain Thorne?"

"Garcia?"

"No, ma'am. Would you like to make an appointment to see the assistant director?"

"Yes."

"How about ten o'clock tomorrow? At the National Defense Agency building in Suitland."

"So this really is a government agency?"

"Yes, ma'am."

"Can you tell me anything about the job?"

"No, ma'am."

"Ten a.m.?"

"Yes."

"I'll be there."

She set the phone down on the counter. Government work. Maybe it wouldn't be so bad. Unless it was a handoff to a contractor who needed a special skill set. But Blunt said he worked there, and he was as regular army as it got. She'd have to see what the offer really was.

She glanced at her watch. Almost six. She looked in the refrigerator and pulled out a number of items to make a dinner salad—lettuce, olives, cherry tomatoes, cucumber, and a cooked chicken breast. While she was making her salad, her smartphone rang. It was a number she didn't know. What the hell. "Hello?"

"Katie, how are you? I was hoping to get in touch. But I thought maybe by now you might have changed your number." It was her ex-husband.

"Why would I do that, Frank?"

"I don't know. I just ... "

"So what's up?" She sliced the chicken breast into strips and fanned it on top of the lettuce, cucumber, and tomatoes.

"I'm in DC this week, and I was wondering if you wanted to get some coffee."

"I'm not going to sleep with you."

"Hey, it's not like that."

"How's your girlfriend? What's her name?"

"Cathy. And she's not my girlfriend, not anymore."

KD set the knife down and opened the jar of olives. "Well, sorry—if that's the right thing to say."

"I made a mistake."

"You weren't a good fit?"

"No. About you. I made a mistake about you."

She walked to the sink and looked out the window at the street down below. The traffic was stop and go. "A little bit late, isn't it?"

"I know."

"I begged you to stay. Promised—hell, I promised so much stuff, I can't even remember."

"I know."

"But you said that you realized that having kids was the most important thing in your life, and if I wouldn't go along, you'd have to leave me no matter how much you loved me."

"I was an idiot."

"I'm not arguing." She gripped the edge of the sink with both hands. "You know what I did?"

"Afterward, with Harry? Yeah, I heard about it. Got to admit I was shaking my head."

"I was a mess."

"Yeah."

"So you still want kids?"

"Not as much as I want you."

A car horn blared. Three sparrows flew off a telephone wire. "Coffee. That's all?"

"Coffee. There's a Caffeination on the corner by my hotel."

"Tomorrow afternoon? Say, five o'clock?"

"Five it is. At the Caffeination next to the Hyatt. See you there."

KD took her salad to the kitchen table, poured a glass of water, and sat down. Did she really want to let him back into her life? Married almost ten years, all they'd been through together, knowing the whole time that she didn't want kids. And then he dropped the bomb. Blew up her life like only he mattered. Why shouldn't she just let him twist in the wind? She ate a bite of salad and chased it with a drink of water. She could ghost him, give him a taste of the rejection she still felt. But she didn't want to. She set down her knife and fork, closed her eyes, and took three deep breaths. Christ, why did she still have feelings for him? Even now, two years later. Well, she wasn't going to let him know how much it still hurt. What was she afraid of? It was only coffee. No reason not to go.

She picked up her knife and fork and started eating again. There was a fifth of vodka in the kitchen. It was late enough now. As long as she stayed in, watched TV, didn't go out, she'd be all right.

THE NEXT MORNING, shortly after 10:00 a.m., KD, all spit shine in her dress uniform, followed a young woman wearing a gray suit down the hallway of the third floor of the National Defense Agency building. The ibuprofen she'd take hadn't quite quelled the pounding behind her left eye. All the office doors were closed except one. The woman stopped at that door. "Director Garcia? Captain Thorne."

A full-figured Latina wearing a black pantsuit with a white shirt stood up from behind her desk. A silver crucifix hung from her neck. "Captain Thorne, glad you could make it."

She reached across her desk to shake KD's hand. "Have a seat."

The office was entirely government issue, with a picture of the president and the agency head on the back wall, but no family pictures or mementos. The top of Garcia's desk was clear except for one file folder and the desktop computer that sat on the right side of her desk.

"Let's get down to business." She opened a document on her computer. "Katherine Denise Thorne, PhD environmental science, captain, United States Army—and you've spent the last four years over at NASA."

"That's all done now."

"Yeah, that affair with your colleague didn't turn out so well."

"That was supposed to be removed from my record."

Garcia patted the paper file in front of her. "It's not in here." She turned back to the computer screen. "We need a certain type of person for this job. Blunt vouched for you, but your record seemed to lack certain details. It took some digging around to find them. Let's talk about how you ended up over at NASA."

"Yes, ma'am."

"At the pickup point after a mission, you disobeyed a direct order to board a chopper and went back for a soldier who'd been left behind providing cover fire."

"He hadn't caught up, and I didn't believe he was dead. I thought the chopper pilot should give him a few more minutes."

"Was he a particular friend of yours?"

"Didn't really know him."

"But you found him wounded, evaded capture, and carried him to a new rally point?"

"I wear the ranger tab. Leave no man behind seems pretty clear to me."

"If you hadn't disobeyed that order, you probably would have gotten a medal for rescuing that man."

"Maybe."

"And then immediately afterward, you applied for the NASA assignment. Why?"

"Wanted to do something different. Get out of the sandbox. Do some science. Work on my marriage."

"Exemplary record before that incident. What do you think your record tells me?"

"You tell me."

"Adrenaline junky, problem solver, idealist—that's why you chose the NASA assignment."

"If you say so."

"Loyal—maybe a little too loyal. You can let your emotions get ahead of you. And smart. That was an impressive PhD dissertation."

"That was a long time ago. Why am I here?"

"You know why you're here. Your boyfriend's wife raised a stink, and NASA didn't want the publicity. So they threw you over. It's bullshit. It's not fair. But that's the way it is. That life is done. Do you want a new life? A life that suits your particular skills?"

"Doing what?"

"I run an investigative unit."

"I'm not interested in law enforcement."

"Neither am I. This is strictly national security investigations. You'd be paired up with Blunt in the field."

"Blunt's a good man, but he can be a pain in the ass."

"Too honest, you mean? He's an excellent field operative. And he'll get you up to speed on tradecraft."

"I'm in charge?"

"You'd be the quarterback, Captain."

"This is a military assignment?"

"If that's how you want it. You come onboard, you'll be reinstated with backpay at your current rank, and you'll be promoted on the usual schedule for officers on special assignment."

"But I won't ever go back on regular assignment?"

"That's over, Captain. There's no way to get there from here. From here on out, it's civilian clothes and my rules if you want to serve your country."

"What are your rules?"

"Get results. Around here we're not so picky about personal behavior. Whatever consensual activities you want to engage in off the clock, that's your business. As long as you do your job and tell me the truth, I don't care who you fight or who you sleep with. Do you want the job?"

"I'll think about it."

"You do that. Clock's ticking."

AT FIVE O'CLOCK, KD pushed through the door of the Caffeination coffee shop next to Frank's hotel. He was already there, sitting at a table in the back. His red hair was a little shorter, his beard a little longer, but he was still built like the rugby player she'd met in college. She wove her way through the other tables and paused a second before she leaned down and pecked his cheek. "Hey," she said, "Let me get some coffee."

When she got back with her latte, she sat to his left, her knees almost touching his chair.

"You look good," he said.

"You, too. Still running?"

"Couple of miles a day."

"Still at Volstagg Engineering?"

"Got a promotion last year. I'm managing a NASA project now."

"Congrats."

"And you're on your own."

"I was offered a job this morning. Not finished thinking about it."

"Do you want to bounce it off me?"

"Are we intimate? I don't remember when you won my trust back."

"I deserve that."

"You do." She sipped her coffee. "So what made you think you made a mistake?"

Frank leaned forward and tried to look her in the eye. "Woke up one morning and realized I was in an alternate reality trying to shape it back into the old reality."

"Meaning?"

"I ran through three girlfriends. All of them smart, pretty, fun. All of them wanting kids in the future. But whenever I was doing something with one of them, I ended up thinking about something else I did with you." He looked past her shoulder at the people standing in line to order. "With the first one, I thought maybe I was still moving on. With the second one, I thought maybe we just didn't quite click at a deep level. And with Cathy, hell, you almost have the same name."

"And the kid thing?"

"I didn't want to have kids with them. I wanted to have kids with you. So if you don't want kids, then I wasn't meant to have kids."

"How do you know I don't have a man?"

"You never were a rebounder, Katie, not even in college. You always processed out of a relationship, took up a new sport, met some new friends. I'm thinking you're still pissed off about Harry."

"You'd be right." She finished her coffee. "So you're thinking you'll take your chances like you did when I broke it off with—God, what was that guy's name?"

"Kyle."

"Yeah, Kyle. What a bastard. First guy I ever punched."

"He had it coming."

"Borrowed my car to cheat on me. We were so young then. Why do you think we always measure ourselves against the one we were dumped for? I didn't punch him for taking the car. I punched him for thinking that he could screw Gemmie and then get back in bed with me."

"How do you think I felt when you took up with Harry after me?"

"I wanted to hurt you, but I mostly hurt myself."

"And his wife."

"No, he did that. He didn't need any help from me."

A woman interrupted them to ask if she could take their extra chair. KD nodded. Frank glanced around the room. "It's getting crowded in here. You want to go to the hotel bar where it's a little quieter, get a drink?"

She shook her head. "I'm trying to avoid drinking."

"Why's that?"

She looked down at her shoes. "I get angry when I drink. Start thinking about things I should forget about."

"Is that how you got the bruises on your hands?"

"You don't know the half of it."

"See, this is what I'm trying to say. See how we just fall back into our relationship, our knowing each other, our history together."

She looked up. "You been to therapy?"

He grinned. "Still going. Look, I want to keep talking. It's early, but we could catch some dinner. My treat."

"I'm still angry at you."

"I know. But you've still got to eat. I want to know all about you."

"It's your dollar."

They went to dinner at the upscale Mexican restaurant on the other side of the hotel. KD explained the repercussions of losing the NASA posting, the civilian job search, and finally the National Defense Agency offer.

"So it's not a normal military posting—"

"No jungle, no sandbox."

"And it's not a science posting—"

"No. I don't think so. Reading between the lines, science might come into it sometimes, but it's national security investigations. Or that's what Garcia says."

"And you don't think it's a pity fuck."

"No, I don't think Garcia is hiring me because she feels sorry for me."

"And you get to keep being a soldier."

"Of sorts."

"What are you going to do?"

"Don't know. Don't want a civilian job."

Frank reached across the table and pointed at the back of her hand. "These bruises. Who have you been fighting? You take up mixed martial arts?"

"I'm embarrassed to say."

"That bad, huh?"

"I had to fight off some guys the other night."

"Fight off some guys?"

"It's the second time that's happened recently."

"The second time? Katie, what the hell are you doing?"

"I don't know. That's the problem. I start drinking and I end up somewhere where bad things can happen."

Tears welled up in his eyes. "Jesus, Katie. How much do you hate yourself? That is so fucking dangerous."

"I know."

He reached for her hand, but she shook her head and pulled away. "What are you going to do now?" he asked.

"I don't know. I just can't drink. I think if I can just get through this rough patch, I'll be all right."

"You shouldn't be by yourself. Do you have someone you can call?"

"No. I don't know anyone here."

"I'm not going to let you do anything to hurt yourself. Come up to my room and sleep on the sofa."

"Nothing's going to happen."

"Nothing's going to happen."

IN THE MORNING, KD woke up on the sofa in Frank's hotel room. He was already up, sitting at the desk, reading emails on his laptop computer. "Hey," she said.

"Hey. How was your sleep?"

"It was good, I think." She was wearing one of Frank's T-shirts and her panties from the day before. She padded off to the bathroom. "Can I use your toothbrush?"

He didn't look up from the computer. "Help yourself."

She went through her bathroom routine and put the T-shirt and her underwear back on before she came back out into the room.

"You got time for breakfast?" Frank asked. "I've got a meeting at nine, but I'm free until then."

"I should probably get going," KD said. She went to her clothes, which she'd laid out on a chair, and turned her back to Frank before she pulled off the T-shirt and put on her bra.

"What are you doing this evening?"

"I don't know yet."

"I'm free every night until Friday."

"Still hoping for a date?"

"Just want to make sure you're all right."

She turned toward him while she was buttoning her shirt. "I think I'm going to be okay. I appreciate that you didn't try to take advantage of me last night."

He stood up from the desk. "I may not have been the best husband, but I hope I was never an asshole."

"You were a pretty good husband, until you weren't."

"Make a decision about the job?"

"I think I'll give it a try."

"Probably a good idea."

"We'll see."

"Can I call you?" Frank asked. "I get up here a fair amount."

"You really want to get back together?"

"I want to try."

"Maybe I'll give you a call on Thursday if I've got something to talk about."

"I'd like that. I love you, Katie. I don't think I ever really stopped."

"Keep saying it and I might start believing it."

2

A month later, KD and Blunt were at the basement shooting range of the National Defense Agency building in Suitland, Maryland, just southeast of Washington, DC, comparing their paper targets. KD laid out three of her targets on the counter and pointed at the bullet holes. "See that? That's shooting. All on center." She pointed at Blunt's targets, where the holes were just slightly off from hers. "Maybe you need glasses, Blunt."

"Paper targets is not running and gunning," Blunt said. "With these new guns, everybody's Deadeye Dick at the range."

"Yeah, yeah."

KD and Blunt ejected the magazines from the Steyr AUG submachine guns they'd been firing and put the guns back into their cases before they left the gun range. "These are excellent weapons," KD said.

"Standard issue for SWAT. Anywhere we go, things heat up, you'll probably have one of these in your hands, or something pretty much like it."

They turned in the machine guns at the armory and took the elevator up to the lobby level. KD's smartphone buzzed. "Text."

She looked at the face of the phone. "Garcia wants us."

Garcia and a nondescript man in a charcoal suit were sitting at the table in the third-floor conference room when KD and Blunt got there. "Where were you?" Garcia asked.

"At the gun range," KD said. "Cell reception is bad down there."

"Need a repeater," Blunt added.

"Sit down," Garcia said. She turned to the Suit.

"Five weeks ago, there was an explosion at a level-four containment storage facility in the Arizona desert. At first the site managers were calling it an accident caused by an electrical fire. But that was wishful thinking. The ATF is investigating, but I'd like fresh eyes on the problem."

"What's stored there? KD asked.

"An assortment of dangerous toxins."

"So you think something was taken?"

"I hope not. But if something was taken, I want to know what, I want to know who, and I want to know why."

"Why not let the ATF handle it?"

"Because this investigation has gone on long enough."

Garcia cut in. "Dig into this. Find out who did it and why. And if anything is missing, find it before it can be deployed."

"The ATF investigator is expecting to hear from you," the Suit said.

THAT EVENING, Allen McCuller, security consultant for BRK Pharmaceuticals Defense division, sat on a folding chair in Martin Jacobs's basement in Franklin Ford, an exurb outside Philadelphia, with a group of men and women dressed in jeans and hunting clothes. The walls were 1970s wood paneling, and the concrete floor was covered with dark green indoor-outdoor carpeting. McCuller was a big guy, ex-military, with a shaved head and some flab around his middle, even though he still worked out.

On the big screen TV at the front of the room, they were watching a video about the genetics of racial purity. Black and brown people were on a spectrum of criminality and stupidity depending on how little white blood they had. They just couldn't help themselves. They were simply inferior. White people who were criminals or incompetents likely had black or brown ancestors. It was all just genetics. The video made no scientific sense at all.

McCuller had been worming his way into this cell of the Patriot Alliance for almost six months. They proved to be, just as he's suspected from their online presence, a group of pathetic, wannabe insurrectionists. At first, no one had been willing to talk to him, but as he started attending activities—paintball, camping, discussions about white supremacy—he'd gained the trust of their leader, Martin Jacobs.

Jacobs stood up at the front of the room as the video came to an end. He was a pudgy, middle-aged man, soft all over. He talked with his hands in his pockets. "There you have it, guys. If you had any doubts, even if you've got some half breeds in your family, those are the facts. They can't help the way they are, and that's why they can't live among us."

After a short discussion, the group broke up. McCuller sidled up to Jacobs as he was unplugging the coffee pot. "Hey, Marty, that was a good presentation."

"Thanks, Allen. Even if you've heard it before, it doesn't hurt to hear it again. You want to take a couple of cookies with you? They'll be stale by next time."

"No, thank you." He glanced around to make sure they were out of earshot of the others. "I just wanted to let you know that our project is still on track."

"That's great. I really appreciate your help. Have you got a firm timeline? We'll need to be ready."

"It's still a little sketchy. As soon as I know for sure, you'll know."

"Great. Anything else?"

McCuller shook his head.

"See you next time."

McCuller walked down the sidewalk to his car parked on the street. This was a firmly middleclass neighborhood. Recent model cars in the driveways. Manicured lawns. Well-kept-up ranch houses. Jacobs was an accountant. A lot of the other guys worked in offices. What did these people have to be angry about? He unlocked his car. Grownups with good jobs playing basement revolutionaries. It didn't make any sense. He looked in his rearview mirror before he pulled away from the curb. But they were perfect for the plan. They were incompetents. They'd create plenty of panic without really doing much harm.

BACK AT THE HOUSE, Jacobs carried the cookie tray and the coffee pot up the stairs and into the 1990s kitchen. A slim, blonde woman with short hair, wearing yoga pants, a scooped-neck top, and a hooded jacket, sat at the kitchen island reading a message on her phone.

"Marie. What a surprise." He set the cookie tray and coffee pot on the counter by the sink. "When did you get here?"

She dropped her phone into her handbag, slid down from her stool, and hugged and kissed him. "I just flew in." She spoke with a vaguely European accent. "I see Allen is still hanging around. You should get rid of him."

Jacobs smiled. "He's going to help us."

"I doubt it. He doesn't fit the profile of someone who could be recruited out of the Patriot Alliance into the Fatherland Volk."

"I agree. But there's no downside for us. He doesn't know anything you can't find out on the website. And he only knows the people who come to the public meetings."

"That doesn't mean he isn't fishing. He might be a government agent."

"I've got some people keeping an eye on him."

"Twenty-four seven?"

"Enough to know who he is and what he does."

"If you say so."

"He doesn't know about us or your people, if that's what you're worried about."

"I've got complete confidence in you, Marty. Otherwise, I wouldn't be here. But a lot of your people haven't really proven themselves yet, and that worries me."

"Marie, either Allen is all talk or he's going to deliver the nerve agent. If he doesn't, we'll tell him he's not welcome anymore. If he does, we'll be able to take our program to the next level."

"If it isn't a sting. Just seems like a pretty big gamble to me."

"We don't have the money to buy the weapons we need, so it's a gamble we have to take. You wait and see. It's all going to work out."

"I hope so."

He took her hand. "How long are you staying?"

"I'm coming and going. I hope that's all right."

"You're always welcome."

THE NEXT MORNING, KD and Blunt sat in their office crowded around KD's desktop computer, talking on an encrypted video call with ATF agent Kenny Lobos, a narrow-faced man with a handlebar mustache. KD sipped her coffee. "Lobos, thanks for getting back in touch."

"No problem. My bosses said full cooperation."

"You're investigating an arson at a level-four containment storage unit?"

"Arson? That's an understatement. Someone bombed the storage unit. Hand-size debris showered the rest of the compound. I got brought in after they decided it wasn't an accident."

Blunt continued. "How is the place guarded?"

"Contracted security on site. They didn't see a thing. Someone cut the perimeter fence to gain entry."

"But there were security cameras?"

"Oh yeah. They'd been compromised. Video from earlier in the evening was copied in to cover up the intrusion."

"So these were pros."

"Looks that way."

"Any leads?" KD asked.

"There's been social media chatter from some radical save-the-planet groups, but I don't believe they had anything to do with it."

"Why not?"

"Because the posts aren't specific enough. Any group that actually did it would be bragging about it."

KD nodded. "So what do you think?"

"I'm going out on a limb here, okay, but I think they blew up the building to cover up a theft. All of the storage units contained the same assortment of toxins, except that one, which also contained a canister of an experimental nerve agent, XP-93."

"You mean like the stuff the Russians put on that dissident's underwear?"

"You'd know better than me. All I know is that nobody wants to talk about the canister. They're all praying it burned up."

"How sure are you?"

"It's just a theory. Look, we haven't found any bits of the nerve agent canister, and the site managers are all rushing around in cover-your-ass mode, but neither of those really mean anything."

"Could you email us what you have?"

"You bet."

KD ended the call. "So what do you think?"

Blunt rolled his chair back from the desk. "Your guess is as good as mine. I don't know Lobos—is his intuition any good?"

"Maybe his report will tell us something more."

LATER THAT DAY, James Dayton, manager of the defense division of BRK Pharmaceuticals, sat across the desk from his CEO, Bob Briggs, at the BRK Pharmaceuticals building in Wilmington, Delaware. Dayton's pudgy face glowed red against his blond hair as if he'd just lost the last of his poker stake.

Briggs continued talking. He was trying to act nonchalant, but his tone carried his judgment. "What can I say, Jim? We've talked about this before. You went big for the nerve agent antidote. I said, who's going to buy it? You said governments, corporations, anybody who's the least bit concerned that the competition is coming for them. Look what the Russians are doing. Well, Jim, it looks like no one's concerned." He reached for his coffee cup, but then pushed it away.

"It's going to happen, Bob."

"Really? How soon?"

"Real soon."

"I told you what you needed to do if you wanted the antidote to be a success. Just a tiny incident that we could leverage an ad campaign on. I even suggested that you use McCuller to get it done. But so far? Crickets."

"We're on it. It's taking more time than we thought. These people we're using aren't employees. We have to make them believe they're helping themselves."

Briggs shook his head. "I'm sorry, Jim. The defense division is bleeding so much cash that the board is considering a new direction. The downsizing will probably be fast-tracked. There won't be any bonuses. I can't even promise that you'll have a job at the end of the year."

"That soon?"

"It is what it is."

"How much time do I have to turn things around?"

"A month, month and a half maybe. After that, there's no stopping the inevitable."

Dayton was fuming as he walked down the hall to the elevators. The news was even worse than he expected. Bob put all the blame on him, even though the whole nerve agent antidote program had been Bob's idea. Dayton punched the button to call the elevator. His timeline to turn everything around was now even shorter than before. The elevator doors opened. The elevator was empty. He got inside. The balloon payment on the mountain cabin was due in six months. His mom was in that expensive care center. Both Janie and Phil were in college. Three more years until he was out from under that. And

Brenda's café was leaking money like a kitchen strainer. Why had he let her talk him into underwriting that fiasco? It had seemed like such a good idea at the time. Her too busy at the café to notice him chasing after that intern.

The elevator opened on the first floor. He was so screwed if he couldn't save his job. The plan had to work. Just a tiny nerve agent incident. That's all they'd need. When the stock price shot up because of the defense division's nerve agent antidote, Bob would take the credit and the board would change its mind. But he'd get his bonus and a raise. His job would be secure. Was there any way to get Allen to speed things up?

HOWARD RAWLINGS STOOD beside his Ford Bronco in the parking lot of a private airfield outside Phoenix, Arizona, smoking a cigarette and watching the door to the administrative building. Even wearing jeans, a golf shirt, and gym shoes he looked like a military man. Allen McCuller came out the door, his suit coat open and his tie loose, sweat glistening on his head, a taped cardboard box under one arm. Rawlings flicked his cigarette onto the pavement and crushed it out.

"How was the drive?" McCuller asked.

"I expected you sooner. I've been in Phoenix a week."

"Relax. It took longer to prep the sample than I expected it to.

"Why's that?"

"First guy backed out. Finding a new guy was complicated."

"This is all taking longer than I thought it would. My guys are expecting to be paid."

"You'll get paid when we get paid, just as we agreed. That's how you end up with a full share."

Rawlings raised the liftback. McCuller set the box down.

"Is the sample good to go?"

McCuller nodded. "It's been aerosolized to expedite the spread."

"This isn't going to cause any blowback, is it?"

"Relax, Rawlings, it's just part of the wargame scenario we're testing. No one's going to die."

"You sure?"

"If you want out, I'll find someone else. You'll be paid for your time, but you'll forfeit your cut."

"I didn't say I wanted out. I asked if you were sure."

"I'm sure, okay? Just do your part."

McCuller walked back into the building. Rawlings closed the lift-back, got into the Bronco, and took out his smartphone to set a course for San Mateo, California. Wargame scenario—that was the lamest cover story he'd ever heard. McCuller was a smug asshole. Taking the nerve agent, testing it out in public, he just hoped McCuller knew what he was doing.

Rawlings took a left out of the parking lot. If he didn't get a big payout from this job, he'd be completely underwater, would definitely lose the house, might even go bankrupt. And his marriage was already a mess. Julie felt abandoned—a pile of unpaid bills and him not there, but what could he do? She knew how he made a living when she married him. And he still didn't trust her, no matter how much she claimed she wasn't cheating. But if the bills were paid, if she knew she could count on him, everything would be different. So he couldn't give up on this payday, no matter how much bullshit came out of McCuller's mouth. Nothing else could turn his life around.

THAT EVENING, back in Washington, DC, KD and Frank were walking on the National Mall after dinner. They'd had supper at an Indian restaurant near a close-by metro stop, and now they were eating ice cream from little cups as they walked along. Frank glanced up at the Washington Monument, which seemed to glow in the spotlights. "Think they'll ever get done working on it?"

"The monument? I gave up on getting to ride up to the top a long time ago."

Some Asian tourists were standing at the construction barrier while one of their number took their picture. KD ate her last spoonful of ice cream and dropped the cup into a trash can. "You haven't said anything about how your project is going."

"Classified."

"Thought it was a NASA project."

"Funded by the DOD."

"So it really is like the old days. Neither one of us can talk about our work."

"But you're doing better? You seem better."

"Yeah. I'm feeling more settled. I've got a place where I belong. My partner is a good guy. I knew him years ago under different circumstance, so it's not like starting from scratch."

"And you're not out tempting fate?"

"I don't know about that. I'm here with you." She motioned with her right hand. "Circle around the monument and walk back the way we came?"

"Sure."

"I want to thank you for looking after me last time."

"Please ... "

"No, really. The anger and the drinking and the loneliness—I was at the edge of the abyss. If I'd continued drinking, I probably wouldn't have taken the job. And then I wouldn't have a place to be and problems to solve."

"You doing anything about the drinking?"

"I went to a few meetings, more for the company than anything else, but you know me. I'm not a joiner. I'm good now. I can keep straight if I've got work. What about you? How's the therapy going?"

"I feel like I'm in a good place, but I'm still going. Don't know if I need it, but I'm just not ready to stop."

"Your insurance is too good."

"You're probably right." He veered off to a trash can to throw away his empty ice cream cup. "Maybe I'll just take a break. See how it goes."

"Dating anyone?"

He shook his head no.

"Thinking about it?"

"I'm waiting for you to say yes."

"You might be disappointed."

"I might be. But I have to know I tried."

She took his hand. "It's good to see you, Frank. But I've got an early morning, so I'm going to take the shortcut back to my car."

"It's always great to see you, Katie."

She squeezed his hand and kissed him on the cheek. "Give me a call the next time you're in town."

MARTIN JACOBS, Olivia Simmons, and Eric Bell sat in a stolen plumber's van on a dark side street in a rundown neighborhood in downtown Franklin Ford. Olivia was a busty blonde who could have passed for a plus-size model. Bell was tall and thin with a lumberjack beard. With them were two new recruits to the Fatherland Volk, Cassie and Rob, a suburban couple Bell met at work and invited to the Patriot Alliance meetings six months ago. They were all wearing dark clothes and had ski masks in their laps. Jacobs spoke to Rob and Cassie. "You saw this neighborhood while we were rolling in here. Trash, dirt, graffiti—air smells like that crap these foreigners eat."

"My grandma used to live down here, if you can believe that," Bell said. "Used to be safe. Used to be clean." He pointed across the street to Ninth Street Falafel. "That falafel place used to be a diner. My gramps used to take me there on Saturday morning."

"These people fuck up everything everywhere they go," Jacobs said. "That's why their countries are so screwed up. Instead of fixing their own, they come here. They steal our jobs. They don't pay taxes. They crowd out needy Americans from the food pantry and the free clinic."

"White Americans," Simmons said.

"And they don't speak English and don't want to learn," Bell said.

"You said you wanted to step up," Jacobs said. "Now's your chance to prove it. Are you ready?"

Rob gripped his wife's hand. "Yes," he said.

Cassie glanced at her husband. She made a fist with her other hand to stop it trembling. "Yes," she said. "We're ready."

"Good," Jacobs said. "The falafel place just closed. Those job stealers will be coming out any minute. We're going to let them know just how we feel."

"Beat the crap out of them," Bell said.

"We know it's hard the first time," Jacobs said. "It's not what we're taught growing up. But you're not alone. That's why we're strong. Who's going to protect our kids?"

"We are," everyone said in unison.

"Who's going to protect our country?"

"We are."

"Okay then," Jacobs continued. "We run across the street, don't stop, don't slow down, hit them before they can run. Then we'll spray paint the windows. I've got a gun just in case things go wrong."

They pulled on their ski masks, got out of the van, and crept to the corner, where they could watch the front of Ninth Street Falafel. Three Middle Easterners, two men and a woman, all wearing cooks' whites, came out. One of the men locked the door.

"Now," Jacobs said.

Jacobs, Simmons, Bell, and the new recruits rushed across the street. Bell knocked the woman down and stepped over her to punch the closest man in the face. Simmons and the recruits swarmed the other man, battering him from all sides.

"Help," the woman yelled. "Help."

"Here's some help." Simmons kicked her in the face.

They beat the two men to the ground. Then they took turns kicking the fallen Middle Easterners while Jacobs sprayed "Sand niggers go home" on the window in red paint.

"Let's go," Jacobs said.

They ran across the street back to where they'd parked the van. Bell climbed into the driver's seat. Everyone else got in the back.

"Drive," Jacobs said. "Drive."

Bell sped away, screeching around the first right turn.

Jacobs pulled off his ski mask. "See how easy that was?"

Rob and Cassie were smiling and nodding. Simmons patted Cassie on the back. "You two did great."

"I was so scared," she said.

"First-time jitters. Next time will be so easy."

"We've got plans, big plans for the future," Jacobs said. "We're going to open everybody's eyes. America's going to be for Americans. And anyone who thinks different can go to hell."

3

The next morning, KD was at her desk, reading ATF Agent Lobos's report on the level-four containment storage unit explosion when Blunt came in, carrying two to-go coffees.

"The man of the hour," KD said.

Blunt handed her one of the cups. "Black, right?"

She nodded.

"What time did you get in here?"

"About an hour ago."

Blunt swung his office chair around and sat down facing her. "You trying to make me look bad? We need to get here about the same time."

"I couldn't sleep."

"I thought you had a date with your husband."

"My ex-husband. And it wasn't a date."

"Did you eat food and talk about personal stuff? That's a date, Doc."

"Wasn't a date. Wasn't romantic."

"Doc, do I know more about relationships than you? You've known this guy a long time. Used to be married. You've had sex and argued and told your deepest secrets. Your heart is not going to go pitter-patter. You're not going to see hearts and butterflies. You're long past that."

"Blunt, I didn't know you were such a relationship expert. Maybe I should call your wife and see what she has to say."

"Don't change the subject. It was a date."

"You're an asshole, Blunt."

"But I'm right. What're you reading?"

"Agent Lobos's report," KD said.

"Anything good?" Blunt swung his chair back around to his desk, input his password on his computer, and found the report.

"Just more details."

"Nobody hurt?"

"No one. All the security personnel were at the other end of the compound."

"So we got nothing?"

"Take a look at the last page. That's where Lobos describes the XP-93 nerve agent."

Blunt scrolled through to the end of the document. "Christ. This stuff is worse than VX. Asphyxiation, convulsions, heart attack, coma. If you don't get the antidote within twelve hours, you're dead."

"And it's possible to aerosolize it."

"Maybe it was destroyed in the explosion."

"Lobos said all kinds of shrapnel rained down. They were picking up pieces all over. If the nerve agent had still been there, some residue should have been on at least one of those pieces."

"So you think Lobos's theory is correct?'

"I hope I'm wrong, but we've got to assume the worst."

"Then we better tell the boss."

KD called Garcia, put the phone on speaker, and filled her in.

"So," Garcia said, "there's no solid evidence that the nerve agent was taken? It's all just Lobos's theory and your speculation?"

"That's it, boss."

"But whoever broke in took control of the security cameras, blew the building without killing anyone, and didn't leave any evidence behind?"

"That's what we've got."

"Then for now we have to assume they took the nerve agent. And you say there're no leads?"

"Nothing."

"Have Agent Han search the database for similar break-ins. See if anything shakes loose."

RAWLINGS SAT FACING out in a parking space at the far end of the rest stop on Interstate 5 near Fresno, the windows down on his Bronco. The day was already hot. Most of the parking spaces were full, and there was a continuous stream of people going in and coming out of the welcome center. He looked back toward the off ramp into the rest stop. O'Malley should have been here by now. Not a good sign. O'Malley had always liked to play things fast and loose, but over the last year it had become a problem. Rawlings was beginning to wonder if he had alcohol or drug issues. Or maybe he just wasn't cut out for the freedom of civilian life. Too many distractions. Not enough structure. Only time would tell.

He heard the tap of a horn. O'Malley, wraparound sunglasses and black T-shirt, was waving at him from a Camry. O'Malley pulled in next to him, got out, and climbed into the Bronco. "Hey, hey," he said.

"I was beginning to think you weren't going to make it," Rawlings said.

O'Malley took off his sunglasses and hung them on the front of his shirt. "Got stuck behind a four-car pileup. Took the cops thirty minutes to clear a lane."

Rawlings reached into the back seat, pulled a backpack up into his lap, and unzipped the main compartment. "Here's everything you need. Facemask, syringe containing the antidote, and the device. You set the straw on the top of the canister upright out of the backpack, you flip the switch, and you're good to go. You want to be in an enclosed space."

O'Malley nodded. Rawlings handed him the backpack.

"Why go all the way to San Mateo? Why not use it here? Tons of people. I could set it in the men's room. Ought to get plenty of casualties."

"Because that's not the plan," Rawlings replied. "We talked about this. We're not trying to maximize the casualties; we're trying to control the number of victims so that no one dies and we can judge how public health officials respond. That's why we want to run this test in a medical facility."

"Just seems like extra trouble."

"Trouble worth taking. So you're going to do this job as planned. You're going to San Mateo to the nursing home where your grandpa lives because no one will stop you from going in or out, and you're going to disperse the nerve agent in a room with two or three healthy people in it. That's all. Can you do that?"

"Yeah, major, I'll get it done."

"Good. Contact me when you're finished."

Rawlings watched O'Malley drive back onto the freeway. Why couldn't he just follow orders? Why did he always have to baby him along with explanations? After they got paid on this job, maybe it was time to cut him loose.

THE NEXT DAY, at noon, McCuller pulled into the parking lot of Ellen's Café, an upscale soup and sandwich restaurant located near the BRK Pharmaceuticals building in Wilmington, Delaware, and parked at the far end of the lot next to Dayton's BMW. Dayton was standing behind his car in the shade of a large maple. "Hey, James," McCuller said.

Dayton nodded. "Was your trip uneventful?"

"No complications. Rawlings has the XP sample."

"So a couple of days?"

"If you still want to go through with it. Once they release it, there's no turning back."

"This test will tell us if the plan is really going to work. If the collateral damage is too high, we'll call it off and find another way."

"How high is too high?"

"Two or three people infected in a health care facility? No one should die. And the pump will be primed so that the authorities will be ready for the main event."

"And if the test pans out?"

"You know all about these Patriot Alliance people, right? They're just play-acting. We give them the nerve agent. They do something stupid enough to dominate the news cycle, the stock jumps, and our jobs are secure."

"If they don't cause a major catastrophe."

"That's one of the reasons we're running the test. We're going to make sure that stupid isn't too stupid. Stock price affected. Nobody hurt. That's our goal."

"What makes you so sure the authorities won't see through this?"

"Allen, how many times have we been over this? We've got nothing to do with the nerve agent. Just the antidote. So we've got no direct connection. That's our cover."

"There's always risk."

"If you've got another way to save our jobs, I want to hear it. Have you got bills? I've got bills. Do you have a future you want to save? I do. Wait and see, this time next year our problems are going to be a distant memory. Now let's go inside and get some lunch."

At 1:00 a.m., a cab dropped Rawlings on the street in front of his house in the Maryland suburbs of Washington, DC. He opened the side door to the two-car garage and rolled his bag around the front of his Dodge truck and his wife's Toyota RAV4 to enter the house through the kitchen. The under-the-cabinet lights were on. All the granite counters were spotless. He set his bag down by the kitchen island, opened the refrigerator, and found the last beer in the back behind the sparkling water. He twisted off the cap and took a long pull. He'd given the nerve agent to O'Malley. Now all he had to do was wait for him to report back.

He glanced toward the stairs. The light had been on in their bedroom when he drove up. Would Julie come down or pretend she hadn't heard him and just turn the light off? The surveillance camera he'd set up in their bedroom hadn't caught her in the act, but that didn't mean anything. He had an intuition that she'd gotten a new boyfriend, even after she'd cried and sworn she'd never do it again.

He took one more pull on the beer before he went up the stairs. Their bedroom door was open, the light streaming into the hallway. He rolled his bag in. "Hey, baby."

Julie put a bookmark in her book. Even without makeup she was something to look at. "Honey. How was your flight?"

"Long." He leaned down to kiss her.

"You need a shave," she said.

"I missed you."

"I missed you, too. Can you tell me where you've been?"

"Classified. But I'm home for a while."

"You going to shower tonight?"

He shook his head.

"Then I'll wait for you." She went back to reading.

He stripped down to his shorts and went into the bathroom to brush his teeth and rinse his face. When he came back out, she closed her book and turned off the lamp on her side table. He turned off the overhead light and got into bed beside her. She took his hand.

"I didn't mean to stay up so late. But I'm glad I did."

"Me, too."

"It's good to have you home."

"You have work tomorrow?"

"Yes, but I'll come home for lunch." She kissed him. "Sweet dreams."

At 4:00 a.m., Rawlings slipped out of bed. Julie was snoring gently. He snuck around the bed and took her phone from her bedside table. Then he crept downstairs to the kitchen, input her password, and scanned through her texts. Nothing unusual. Emails, also innocent. Then he opened her photos. Two recent selfies. Naked. All of her displayed to advantage. They definitely made him want to fuck her, but they hadn't been sent to him. So were they originally for him, and she'd changed her mind about sending them? Or was she deleting the incriminating texts that went with these pictures?

He closed the phone. Her shoulder bag was sitting on a chair by the back door. He pulled out her laptop computer, opened it on the kitchen counter and input her password. He went into her work email. Lots of emails from Patrick. Rawlings thought for a minute. He smiled. Oh, yeah. Older gay guy who likes his wine. Agency partner or something. Wait a minute. Two Patricks here. Fewer emails from him, though. He closed the laptop and put it back into her shoulder bag before he crept back up the stairs with her phone. Two pictures. That was all. No way to be certain. He needed to run a retrieval program on the phone and the computer, see what she'd deleted. To do that, he'd need twenty or thirty minutes uninterrupted.

When he woke up at 8:45 a.m., she was already gone. He checked his surveillance camera setup. All good. He did a walk-through of the house, looking for anything that might mean a man had been inside, but the house was as clean as if the cleaners had been there yesterday. Maybe he needed a second camera in the spare bedroom. Maybe they were fucking in the living room.

A place was set at his usual spot at the kitchen island with a note lying on the plate. *Honey, your breakfast is warming in the oven.* He opened the oven. She'd made him an egg casserole, the one with sausage and mushrooms. He went to the coffee maker. It was loaded and ready to go. All he had to do was push the button. Maybe he was being an idiot. Maybe she really was glad to see him.

After he ate and put his dishes in the dishwasher, he shaved, showered, and put on sweatpants and a T-shirt. He was sitting in the living room reading the newspaper on his laptop when she hurried into the house at noon.

"Come on, no time to waste, I've got a one-thirty meeting." She ran up the stairs.

By the time he got to their bedroom, she was naked, her clothes lying haphazardly over the chair by her dresser. "Hurry up," she said.

He pulled his T-shirt over his head. She tackled him. He staggered back against the wall. "You okay?" she laughed.

He tossed his shirt free. She boosted herself up, locked her legs over his hips, and kissed him hard. "I missed you so much." She kissed him again, her arms around his neck. "I wanted you last night, but I was too tired."

He carried her to their bed, tossed her onto the bedspread, pulled off his sweatpants, and climbed up after her. "You think you were tired last night. You'll have to take the afternoon off."

"You think so? Come get me."

Afterward, they ate sandwiches in the kitchen. "How's business?" Rawlings asked.

"That million-dollar house I've been trying to close? I'm pretty sure that's going to happen this afternoon."

"So that's why you're flying high."

She patted his hand. "Just happy to see my baby." She drank some sparkling water. "But I don't want to screw this up. We need the cash."

"I know. I've got a payday coming, too, but I'm just not quite sure when."

"That's the problem with both of us being self-employed."

"We'll get some savings in the bank pretty soon."

She glanced at the clock on the stove. "Got to go."

He stood to kiss her. "Good luck."

She hurried out the door. He waited until he was sure she was at the end of the block before he got into his truck and went after her. So exuberant. So happy to see him. So positive about their financial situation. Was she really that easy to read?

He caught up to her when she was a few blocks away from the real estate office. Traffic was busy so he fell in two cars behind. She pulled into the real estate office parking lot and rushed into the building. He parked across the street. Why was he even bothering today? Could she possibly be that committed to someone else? He had been gone more than he'd been home over the last few months, but still, going from him to another man in the same afternoon?

She came out by herself and drove away. He followed. She went across town and into a new development of huge houses situated around a man-made pond, where she pulled into a house with one of her *For Sale* signs in the yard. A Porsche SUV was parked in the driveway. When Julie got out, her bag over her shoulder, a middle-aged man and woman wearing golf clothes got out of the Porsche. Rawlings kept driving. Nothing to see here. Maybe he was just paranoid. But the pictures were definitely suspicious. He needed to look at her deleted texts and emails. Who did he know who could supply him with a retrieval program, no questions asked?

He drove back toward his house. He needed to keep his head in the game. There was still business to take care of. O'Malley was supposed to disperse the nerve agent. When he left him, he was only a few hours away from San Mateo. Why hadn't he heard back from him yet? He pulled into a convenience store parking lot and got out his burner phone. O'Malley answered on the third ring.

"I was wondering why I hadn't heard from you."

"No worries, Major, I'm doing this job right. Just like you wanted. You'll be hearing from me in the next day or two."

That evening Rawlings and his wife ate at a steak house across from the megamall and then took a walk through the neighborhood, holding hands. A few neighbors out walking dogs said hello or waved from across the street.

"It's good to be home," Rawlings said.

"You've been gone so much, it's like I don't know what to do," Julie replied.

"You'll just have to get used to me being in the way."

She bumped up against his shoulder. "I don't think that will be a problem."

"Good. I love you."

"I love you, too."

Rawlings slipped out of bed at three-thirty, took Julie's phone again, and crept down to the living room, where he plugged her phone into his laptop. An old buddy from the sandbox, a tech head who worked private now, had dropped him a retrieval program. He found Julie's nude pictures on her phone, opened the retrieval program on his computer and let it do its job. Both pictures had been texted on different dates to the same phone number. Rawlings wasn't surprised, but he was disappointed. She'd always been unfaithful. Loved him and been unfaithful. Would it have been any different if he was home all the time? If they had a family?

He had to stop beating himself up. Lots of wives made friends, joined clubs, found some way to keep busy while their husbands were deployed. He exited the retrieval program. What was he going to do now? Was she done with this guy now that he was home? Was he going to pretend? He put away his laptop, went back upstairs, put her phone back, and climbed into bed. She snuggled next to him. "There you are," she murmured.

"I'm right here. Go back to sleep."

She sighed. He felt her warmth against him. He had to know who this guy was, if this relationship was just a stopgap, or if he needed to do something about it.

In the morning, Rawlings used the text message phone number to find a name and address. Raul Benson. 2875 Rodeo Avenue. Loan officer at Crystal Savings and Loan. He found a picture of the guy on the saving and loan's website. Chubby, balding, eager to serve. Is that what Julie was looking for?

He drove by Benson's house in the afternoon. Well-maintained two story in a neighbor of similar houses. Suburban in the driveway. Petite, dark-haired woman gardening in a flowerbed in the front. Did she even suspect that her domestic bliss was a scam? A little boy ran down the front steps, pointed at the house, and started talking before the woman even turned her head. So there were at least two kids. Complete domestic tranquility. He called Benson's phone number at the bank. The phone kicked over to voice mail. He was gone for the day. But he wasn't here. He called Julie's cell. It went straight to voice mail. Rawlings gritted his teeth. Careful, careful. This was no time for anger. There'd be plenty of time for that later. Right now he needed to know just how bad things were.

McCuller sat at the bar of a hotel bistro in Philadelphia, sipping on a gin and tonic and watching the women. There was a woman he met here before that he hoped to meet again. Dark haired, curvy, old enough to really know her trade, and not afraid to go into a hotel room on her own. It just wasn't sexy if the girl seemed wary. She had to be confident enough in her own judge of character to know she'd be paid and wouldn't be hurt. He was looking for uncomplicated straight sex, not some creepy domination thing.

Thus far, he'd noted two promising candidates, a blonde and a Latina, but they were skittish, probably trying to decide if he was a cop. That was the problem with being a security professional. The cop vibe. He sipped his drink. He was staying the night, didn't have to be in a hurry, wanted to make sure he really got something special.

Just as he was about to order a fresh drink, he felt a tap on his shoulder. There she was, his dark-haired beauty. She was wearing a teal cocktail dress with a pendant on a gold chain that hung down to her cleavage. "Surprised to see me?" she said.

"Yes, I am. Have you got time for me this evening?"

"We've got all the time in the world."

He turned to the bartender. "Put my tab on my room."

They left the bistro arm-in-arm, cutting across the lobby to the elevators. "There's white wine in the minibar."

"Can't wait."

"Wasn't sure that I'd see you again."

"A guy like you, a guy I know, can always make an appointment." They got into the elevator. "I'll give you my card."

She took a business card out of her clutch purse. A phone number was printed on one side, the other side was blank. He slipped it into his front pocket.

They got off the elevator and strolled down the hall to his room. Once inside, she set her purse on the desk and slipped off her high heels. "Same rate as before, unless you want something different."

He laid $200 on the desk next to her purse. She unzipped her dress and stepped out of it. "Let me help you with your clothes."

. . .

SIMMONS WATCHED Allen and the prostitute cross the lobby and get into the elevator. Simmons was wearing a dark, shoulder-length wig and black framed glasses. No reason to follow Allen any longer tonight. She got up from the chair in the lobby where she'd been sitting pretending to look at her phone and walked outside. What was up with that guy? He wasn't married. Why didn't he just go on a dating website? He looked like a regular guy, but he must be messed up in some way. Rather pay straight up than get to know somebody. Or did he just believe he couldn't date a woman that young and good-looking? Maybe he just didn't want to have sex with someone his own age. Weird.

She walked down the street to the parking deck where she'd left her car. She had her hand on the pepper spray in her handbag, even though there was no one suspicious on the street. She wasn't sure why Marty wanted Allen followed—he didn't act like a cop—but Marty was insistent that he wanted the job done right. She wondered when Marty would be satisfied that he had enough information about Allen's associations. Besides the hookers, he was completely boring.

LATE THE NEXT MORNING, O'Malley walked through the automatic doors of the Sunny Dale Nursing Home in San Mateo, California, with the backpack over one shoulder. He stopped at the counter to sign in and took a right down the hallway to his grandpa's room. His grandpa was lying on his bed fully clothed, napping, his mouth hanging open. The TV, the sound low, was tuned to a news channel. O'Malley watched his grandpa sleep. There was no reason to wake him. He hadn't recognized any of his family members in over three years.

After a few minutes, O'Malley looked at his watch. The two on-site physical therapists would be in their office in thirty minutes. An aide would be here to take his grandpa to the dining room in about an hour. He patted his grandpa's hand before he slipped out of the room. He'd disabled the hallway security cameras shortly after 5:00

a.m. that morning. The hallway was empty. Half the residents were in the dining room for the first lunch shift, and the aides were hovering around to be of service. He went down to the physical therapy offices, opened the door, and looked around the space. Two stationary bikes, three physical therapy tables, a rack of weights, and a desk with a computer on it. This would fit the bill. He walked around the room closing the air-conditioning vents. Then he set the backpack on the floor in the center of the room, put on the facemask, and put the syringe in his shirt pocket before he raised the straw on the device and flipped the switch. As soon as he heard the pressure release from the canister, he backed quickly away, pulled off the facemask as he stepped back out into the hall, and closed the door to the office. He glanced at his watch. The physical therapists should be there in ten minutes.

He walked into the visitors' restroom, put the facemask in the trashcan, and injected himself with the antidote. Whatever was going to happen was going to happen. There was no reason for him to stay.

He texted for a rideshare, walked out in front of the nursing home, and rode to the Hilton out by the Oakland International Airport, where he went to his room, stripped off his clothes into a black trash bag, and showered. Then he packed his duffel, checked out in the lobby, and drove his car into a county park, where he left the trash bag in a trashcan. A group of young men and women were playing volleyball. Several people were walking dogs. Three women were hanging a birthday banner at a shelter, while two men carried coolers from a minivan. He texted Rawlings. *All done.* Rawlings texted back with a thumb's up.

MCCULLER WAS IN AN ACE HARDWARE, picking up a cartridge to fix a leaky faucet, when he got the mission complete text from Rawlings. He paid for the cartridge and got back in his car before he called Dayton. "We're all set."

"Are you sure?"

"Yes. The test run is underway."

"So we'll know in the next twenty-four hours."

McCuller watched a mom and dad with two kids crossing the parking lot. "Hope nothing goes wrong."

"Nothing's going to go wrong."

RAWLINGS CLOSED his message app and put his phone in his pocket. He was parked across the street from the real estate office, waiting for Julie to come out. He'd been tailing her all day in a rented Toyota Corolla to make his job easier. She'd shown two houses and had gone to lunch with a real estate friend, a woman he vaguely remembered having met.

She came out of the building and got into her RAV4. He followed her back across town to the million-dollar house in the new development. She parked in the driveway and went inside. A few minutes later a Cadillac pulled in and parked beside her. Raul Benson, hurrying along, no bounce in his step, no eagerness. Maybe he was just a good actor.

Rawlings got out of the Corolla with his digital camera, looked up and down the street, and casually crossed to the million-dollar house as if he had business there. He avoided the front windows, glanced into the side windows as he walked around back—open floor plan, no furniture, no one visible. Kitchen and family room empty. He squatted to see into an egress window. Basement appeared empty. They must be upstairs. He was beginning to feel stupid crazy, but he had to know.

He went back around to the front and tried the door. Unlocked. He eased the door open enough to pass through. The downstairs was completely quiet. He slipped off his shoes and crept up the carpeted stairs, walking on the edges of the steps so that they wouldn't creak. The door to the nearest bedroom was wide open. He took a quick peek. Empty. The next bedroom was the same. But now he could hear moaning. He crept to the third bedroom. There she was, lying on her back on the carpet, Benson's fat ass pumping up and down, her eyed closed, moans slow and guttural.

He wanted to kill the guy—rip him off her, strangle him, and throw him out the window. He stepped away from the door, took some breaths. It wasn't about that asshole and his wretched marriage. It was about Julie, what she'd promised, how she'd lied, and what he had to do. He checked his camera to make sure the flash was off, stepped back to the door and shot three quick pictures. Then he walked back down the hall as he checked them. Bad angle, not quite focused, but good enough. There was no deniability.

He took the rental car back and went home. He thought about packing his bags and leaving, not even writing a note, hiring a lawyer, dragging her through the media, ruining her career. His phone rang. It was Toms. He steadied his voice. "What's up?"

"Bills are piling up. I know this job has to run its course before we get paid, but do you have any idea when that's going to be?"

"I'm in the same boat with you, brother. Just hang on. As soon as I know anything, I'll let you know."

"Okay."

"How are things otherwise?"

"Other than my wife pissed at me for being gone and the bills not being paid, I'm bored. Can only play driveway basketball with the kids so many afternoons, know what I mean? Do I need another job to tide me over?"

"I'll get back to you."

"I'll be waiting."

Rawlings ended the call. Why couldn't one part of his life work out—his marriage fucked, his business fucked. He needed a real war so he could get out of here and get to a place where things made sense. He changed into workout clothes and went down to the basement gym to work the heavy bag. A fat bald guy. Why did it hurt so much? And what was it with her moaning? He couldn't get it out of his mind.

Rawlings was sitting at the kitchen island, showered and changed, when Julie came into the house at 5:00 p.m. His roller bag sat on the floor by the back door.

"Whoa, baby," she said. "That's your serious face. What's up?"

"Have a seat," he said.

She sat at the island opposite him. "I thought you were going to be home for a while."

"I thought so, too."

He set three photographs on the counter.

She picked up the first one. It was her and Raul in the bedroom of the For-Sale house. She glanced up at Howard. His eyes were staring through her. She picked up the next photo, glanced at it, dropped it on the counter. "You were following me."

"Wasn't any more difficult than the last time."

"I—I don't know what to say."

"You promised me. I trusted you."

She slipped down from her stool. He grabbed her wrist.

"Let go. You're hurting me." She started to cry.

His voice was flat. "I'm the one who's supposed to be crying. I'm the one who's been betrayed."

"Oh, my God." She jerked loose and ran out into the garage. He caught up to her as she was pulling the RAV4's door open, got his arms around her, and carried her back into the house as she struggled to get free.

"Oh no, oh no, oh no. I can explain. It's not what it looks like. It's not what it looks like. I only love you."

He tossed her down on the sofa in the living room. "You've got a strange way of showing it." He got down on his knees in front of her and gripped both her hands. He looked in her eyes. "Whatever you say now had better be the truth."

She looked down in her lap, choking out the words between sobs. "You were gone. We didn't have any money. I couldn't pay the bills—"

"But you've been selling houses—"

"The market is crazy around here. My sales kept falling through at the last minute because of the financing. I needed a loan officer who would see things my way."

Rawlings let go of her hands. "So you started fucking Benson."

"I knew he was interested. So I started flirting with him. I thought that would be enough to get his help."

"But it wasn't."

"I didn't plan anything. It just got to the point where I knew that if I didn't take the next step, I wouldn't get his help with the loan. It was so hard to sleep with him the first time. But I had to make a sale."

He stood up. "Why didn't you tell me things were so bad?"

"Tell you? You knew. You knew we were broke, living off the credit cards. Half the time, I couldn't even get in touch with you."

He tossed her his handkerchief. She mopped her face. "You were so angry. I thought you were going to hurt me."

"I'm still angry. But I would never hurt you. You've got to believe me. When I saw you screwing that guy on the carpet in that empty house, making that animal noise ... "

"My fake orgasm. You heard that? My God." She covered her face with her hands.

He paced back and forth in front of her, not saying a word.

Finally, she said, "What are you going to do?"

"I don't know."

"Are you leaving?"

"No." He sat down beside her. "I've got too many feelings. I'm angry. I feel like a fool. And I feel like I failed you. I'm supposed to take care of you. I'm supposed to keep you safe. I didn't do my job, and that's why you betrayed me."

She shook her head. "I'm so sorry. I didn't want to hurt you. I felt so guilty."

"We've got to do better." Rawlings looked off at the fireplace, the unburned wood he'd stacked there last fall. "So you and Benson, was that quid pro quo? Or was it more like an affair?"

"You really want to hear this?"

He nodded.

"It started sort of like we were helping each other, but now it's sex for every closing."

"So he's a dirt bag who's got you under his thumb."

"It doesn't matter. I'm not doing it anymore."

"You got that right. We've got the photos. He's going to help you for free, and if he whines his wife gets the photos."

"But that's blackmail."

"That's exactly what he's doing to you."

"I don't know, Howie."

"I want to make things right with you. Do you want to make things right with me?"

"Yes."

"Then do it. Just for now, until we get back on our feet. Before the next closing, you give him a photo and tell him how things are going to be."

"Okay, but just until we get our bills paid."

"That's all I'm asking."

She took his hand. "I really meant it the last time, honey. I really meant it when I said I wouldn't cheat on you. You're the only one who has my heart." She started crying again.

He took her hand in his and saw that her wrist was bruised. "Julie, I didn't mean to hurt you. I didn't know. I'm so sorry." He took her in his arms. "We're going to get through this. We're going to make it like this never happened."

4

The next day, all the news outlets were covering the nerve agent attack at the Sunny Dale Nursing Home in San Mateo, California. Three people had been hospitalized, and a five-year-old boy had died. TV doctors were being interviewed about the symptoms of nerve agent exposure and when to seek medical attention. Talking heads were hypothesizing about possible future attacks and foreign government involvement. The CEO of BRK Pharmaceuticals was confident about its ability to meet any possible demand for its top-rated antidote. Rawlings turned off CNN, went to the living room windows and looked out across his front yard. What a fucking mess. He got out his McCuller phone.

"Where are you calling from?" McCuller asked.

"Burner phone."

"So what's this about? You weren't supposed to call."

"You said no one would die."

"Look, I'm as surprised as you. It was a terrible accident. A tragedy for that family. But it doesn't change anything."

"That's bullshit. If I'd known there was going to be so much publicity, that pictures of that little kid would be plastered all over the TV—"

"Who do you think you're fooling? The publicity was the whole point. The authorities figuring out it's the stolen nerve agent—that's what makes the rest of the project work."

"The feds are going to be all over this."

"You didn't release the nerve agent yourself, did you?"

"No."

"How well do you trust the guy you sent?"

"All my guys are top-level operators."

"Then what do you have to worry about?"

"This job is dragging on too long."

"Relax. The pieces of the puzzle are falling into place. Things are going to start speeding up soon. The hard part is over." McCuller ended the call.

Rawlings glanced at his watch. The phone call wasn't long enough to trace. He put the burner phone back in his pocket. Was the hard part over? Or had O'Malley screwed the pooch? Done something that could cause him to be identified? If he had, he could already be under surveillance. Wasn't worth the risk of calling him now. A kid dead. He wished he could have sent Toms or Sebold— they didn't make mistakes—but O'Malley was the one who had access to the right kind of facility. However it played out now was the way it played out. He'd just have to do whatever it took to straighten things out if they went sideways.

"What are you looking at?" Frank asked.

KD blanked the screen on her smartphone and slipped it into her pocket. "Just some work stuff. Has to do with the nerve agent outbreak."

"You're not supposed to be working now."

"I know. I've got a bad habit of checking notifications."

"Tell me about it. I had to turn all of mine off."

They were walking down the sidewalk toward Frank's hotel. There were still plenty of people on the street, entering or leaving restaurants, or hurrying off in rideshares or cabs. They'd eaten at a new American restaurant. Her porkchop had been juicy, but the crème brûlée hadn't been crunchy enough on top. Frank took her hand, and she didn't pull away. They'd been having some fun times together. She was glad he had called her up that day, helped her through that rough night, hadn't tried to have sex. And they'd been going out long enough now that she was falling back into all her old feelings about him—the feelings she'd had before he left her. At a moment like this, she actually had to think to remember why she'd been so angry with him. His betrayal still hurt, but the hurt seemed muted, as if the feeling was somehow separated from what had really happened.

She smiled. "Still no girlfriend?"

"I was hoping I had one here."

"Maybe you do." She turned and kissed him.

"Whoa. That was a surprise."

"A good one, I hope."

They started walking again.

When they got to his hotel, he kissed her hand. "Always so much fun," he said. "I'm out of here tomorrow. Will I see you next time?"

"You going to ask me up?"

He let go of her hand and walked around in a circle. "You sure you're ready? I don't want to go one step forward and two steps back."

"I'm not promising mind-blowing make-up sex, but, yeah, I think I'm ready."

"Want to stop at the bar?"

She shook her head. "I'm going to do this sober, like we used to. Besides, if I start drinking, I might change my mind, and I don't want to change my mind."

He held the hotel's heavy glass door open for her and then led her across the lobby. In the elevator, they kissed, holding each other tenderly, until the doors opened on his floor.

"Still want to?" he asked.

"Yes."

He reached for her hand. "Come on."

KD's PHONE alarm woke her. She was lying in the hotel room bed, Frank spooned around her. She turned off her alarm and sat up off the edge of the bed, naked, her hair loose around her shoulders.

Frank put his hand on her thigh. "Do you have to go?"

She leaned over to kiss him. "I'm glad I came up."

"Stay a little longer."

"I have to go home to change clothes before I go to the office. But if you hurry, I have time for breakfast."

She went into the bathroom, leaving the door open, and turned on the shower. She felt hopeful, more hopeful than she had in a long time. But she wasn't sure if she should trust that feeling. She'd always felt safe with Frank, always felt like she knew where she stood, and then he'd blindsided her. She wasn't going to go through that again. She got into the shower and started washing herself. She could hear Frank at the sink.

"Leave the shower on when you're done."

"Okay."

She came out of the shower dripping. He handed her a towel, kissed her, and got into the shower. It was too easy, she thought. Way too easy to fall back into all the old patterns. She couldn't be sure just yet if they were really going to work out. He was still on his best behavior. Hell, she was still on *her* best behavior. It was like they were on vacation whenever he came to town. She had to be careful.

THREE DAYS after the nerve agent release, Dayton sat at his computer studying BRK's stock price. It had gone up initially, but not as much as he had hoped. Now it was starting to go back down. He called McCuller. "Can you talk?"

"Yes."

"Time to implement the plan."

"Look, I've been toeing the line with Rawlings, but do you really want to do this?

"We can't back out now."

"What about the kid who died?"

"We didn't want that to happen, but there's nothing we can do about it now."

"That's harsh."

"It's a fact. Now's the time to act, while the government is still on alert and people are less likely to be harmed. Give the nerve agent to your contact in the Patriot Alliance. We've got to move quickly if we want to save our bonuses."

"What if this goes wrong? How many more people could die?"

"You told me these Patriot Alliance people were incompetent."

"Completely. That's my point. Anything could happen. What if they release all the XP at one time?"

"Look, if they're stupid enough to release everything at once, and the public really is at risk, we'd tip off the CDC. We're trying to make money, not hurt people."

"You'd really do that?"

"Yes."

"I've been keeping an eye on the BRK price. It didn't go that high."

"But it went high enough. And the nerve agent story was on all the cable news shows. Facebook and Twitter were going crazy. Wait until you see what happens the next time."

"I can't argue with what you're saying. I just don't want to be responsible for any more deaths."

"The reason the price didn't go higher was because of the speed of the public health response. Very few people are going to get contaminated by the nerve agent. We'll get panic, a couple of people will end up in the hospital, the media will go crazy, we'll sell a lot of nerve agent antidote on the fear, the board will change their minds, and we'll save our jobs. This plan is going to work. The worst that could happen is that the Patriot Alliance people might contaminate themselves, and I'm sorry, but I don't care. Give them the nerve agent."

"Okay, I'll do it."

"You won't regret this."

MARIE ADAMESCU and Martin Jacobs were sitting against the headboard of Jacobs's bed, watching the late news roundup on a large TV that hung on the opposite wall. Half the news was about the nerve agent attack in San Mateo. Adamescu reached for her cigarettes. "Not in here," Jacobs said.

She lit a cigarette anyway. "Open the window."

"Christ, Marie." He got up and opened the window.

She ashed her cigarette into an empty Coke can. "That nerve agent attack is no accident."

"You think Allen had something to do with it?"

"Don't you?"

"I'm not arguing," Jacobs replied.

"I told you he couldn't be trusted. No one gives away valuable commodities, no matter their politics. The pharma people are up to something. They plan to use you for a scapegoat."

"What do you think their plan is?"

"It's got to be about making money."

"So you think Allen—"

"And his friends. He's not working alone."

"So Allen and his friends are making money on this deal?"

"Allen acts like he's a true believer, like he's going to prove himself by providing this material, but we don't know where this stuff comes from, and we don't really know who he is. I don't think he's a cop, but he is definitely not one of us. This is the only explanation that makes sense."

"Well, we certainly can't take the nerve agent now. Too much risk."

Adamescu dropped her cigarette into the Coke can and set it on the bedside table. "Maybe we can help each other."

"How's that?"

"You need guns and explosives to advance your work, but you've been having trouble raising the money. Maybe we could make a trade. My people could make use of the nerve agent."

"What would you do with it?"

"Who knows? Don't concern yourself. We'll take it out of the US. It'll be used elsewhere. It will never blow back on you."

"But if we accept delivery from Allen, there'll be a trail from him through us to you."

"Then Allen will have to disappear. And his boss, too, just to be sure."

"I'll think about it."

"You'll get the guns you need."

"It's tricky."

"How will you raise the money? That's the problem with every Fatherland Volk group working independently. It's hard to make large purchases."

"It also makes us impossible to snuff out."

"But right now you need weapons and explosives to do your work and gain members. Weapons you can't afford. Trading the nerve agent could jumpstart your plans. Scaring a few immigrants only goes so far. You've still got your people watching Allen?"

"Yes."

"So he delivers the material. Your people kill him. You can do that, can't you?"

"Sure."

"Make it look like a street crime."

"What about his boss? We don't even know who he is."

"We'll take care of him. You'll get your gear, and our relationship will be closer than ever. You think about it, and I'll talk to my people."

"The guns and explosives? Detonators as well?"

"Of course. Make a list. We'll give you a fair trade."

Jacobs turned off the TV and slid down in bed. "That's a lot to think about."

"You can do that thinking later." Adamescu pulled her nightgown off over her head and straddled him.

"Are you going to leave the lights on?" he asked.

"You don't want to look at me?"

He reached for her. She grabbed his wrists and held them down on either side of his head, bent down as if to kiss him, and bit his lip. Then she whispered in his ear. "What are you going to do to me, Mister? Tell me every dirty detail."

IN THE MORNING, after Jacobs left for the office, Adamescu poured another cup of coffee, sat down at the kitchen island, and took out a burner phone.

"Hey, it's me. You know the relationship I've been working on?"

"The Fatherland Volk? I thought they couldn't put the money together."

"They've got a line on some sort of nerve agent."

"The chemical weapon we've been hearing noise about?"

"It must be."

"So what's your plan?"

"If they can get the material, we trade for the weapons they want. Then we sell the nerve agent to the Muslim radicals I've been working in France."

"I get it. The Muslims use the nerve agent, take credit for the attack, and we push the French government to the right in the next elections."

"Exactly. No more immigration."

"So what will you need?"

"I'll send the weapons list via encrypted email. When the time comes, I'll need the weapons and a private plane to get the nerve agent out."

"Everything will be ready. Keep me informed."

"The timeline isn't certain yet, but as soon as I know, you'll know."

She ended the call. She hoped everything went according to plan. Marty's Fatherland Volk cell could be an important ally in a few years' time. In the meantime, she needed to find out everything she could about Allen's boss.

· · ·

KD AND BLUNT were on an encrypted video call with Dr. Sharon Schwartz, a college buddy of KD's who worked at the CDC. "There's no doubt?" KD asked.

"The nerve agent from the San Mateo outbreak exactly matches the XP-93 that was stored at the Arizona facility," Dr. Schwartz said.

"It isn't different in any way?" Blunt asked.

"It's the exact same formula."

"Thanks, Sharon," KD said.

"Any time, Katie."

KD ended the call.

"So now we know for sure," Blunt said. "Somebody stole the nerve agent."

"And they're using it," KD replied.

"But why release it at a nursing home? What's the point? And nobody's demanding money or taking credit."

"Did the FBI tech guy get back to us?"

"Yeah," Blunt said. "I've got his number right here."

KD set up another encrypted video call.

"Special Agent Simms? Glad we caught you in the office. We understand that you have something for us."

"Surveillance cameras in the hallways of the nursing home had been knocked out, but they forgot about the cameras on the street in front on the building. Let me pull up what we found."

A grainy video showed a man in cargo shorts going into the nursing home with a backpack over his shoulder. When he came out, he wasn't carrying the backpack. "That's the backpack we found in the physical therapy office."

"Are you sure?" KD asked.

"Pretty sure. The footage was hard to clean up."

"Did you get a good enough look at the guy to make an ID?" Blunt asked.

"Yes, indeed. He signed in to visit his grandfather, if you can believe that. He's ex-military. Works for a contractor outfit. He stayed overnight at a Hilton at the airport."

"Any fingerprints on the backpack?"

"No luck."

"Well, at least we've got the guy. Can you email all the info?"

"You bet."

KD ended the call. "What do you think?"

"This guy's worth talking to in person," Blunt said.

THE NEXT AFTERNOON, KD and Blunt rolled into a trailer court at the edge of a small town outside of San Antonio, Texas. Some of the mobile homes had porches and car ports built onto them and roses growing along the front. Others were rusty hulks with concrete block steps, their tiny yards dirt and dry weeds. KD glanced back and forth as she drove. "Which one is ours?"

"Should be the next on the right," Blunt replied.

She pulled their rental Nissan to the side of the gravel street in front of a single-wide trailer with a small porch. A Jeep sat in the driveway and a canoe lay tipped over beside it.

Blunt banged on the door. "Mr. O'Malley," he yelled.

A big man wearing jeans and a black T-shirt opened the door.

"Are you Bill O'Malley?" Blunt asked.

"Who's asking?"

Blunt held up his ID. "We've got a few questions."

"Fire away."

"Can we come in?"

"No."

"Were you in San Mateo, California, last week?"

O'Malley shook his head. "My grandpa is in a nursing home there, but I wasn't there last week."

"What do you do for a living, Mr. O'Malley?"

"Military contractor."

"Who do you work for?"

"Accelerated Results Associates."

"What's the scope of your work?"

He smiled. "You'd have to ask my boss about that."

"Do you currently have any travel plans?"

He shook his head.

"Got a deployment coming up?"

"Not that I know of." He looked from Blunt to KD. "We done here? I've got things to do."

"So you weren't in San Mateo last week?" KD asked.

"Nope."

KD and Blunt got back into their sedan, KD behind the wheel. "That guy isn't a good liar."

"Isn't trying," Blunt said. "Doesn't think we're worth the trouble. Let's see where he goes."

They parked on the shoulder of the road half a block down the street, where they had a good view of the mobile home park's entrance. A few minutes later, O'Malley's Jeep came out the park and turned right. They followed. He took a left at the first traffic light, drove the speed limit for three blocks, turned right, drove past a heating and cooling contractor, and turned into Donny's Auto Salvage. But instead of parking in front, he started down the gravel driveway that ran along the outside of the chain-link fence that surrounded the property.

KD glanced at Blunt. He shrugged. "He already knows we're following him, so we might as well." They continued after him. At the back of the property, O'Malley left the driveway and drove off across an open field, navigating through the dry brush and weedy saplings until he drove down a slope to a shallow creek. After he climbed up the low bank on the other side, he circled the Jeep around to face them and honked his horn and waved before he turned and disappeared over a hill.

KD and Blunt sat at the back of the auto salvage property watching him.

"Not even pretending to be innocent," Blunt said. "He just straight-out ran."

"Well, he's not flying or renting a car, not on his own ID," KD replied.

"That boy?" Blunt replied. "I bet he's got a pocketful of passports."

"Guess we better give his boss a call. Find out what he knows."

O'MALLEY BOUNCED across a ditch and back onto a gravel road near a ranch house two miles across country from Donny's Auto Salvage. A dog was barking from the yard and there were two trucks in the driveway, but he didn't see anyone. He turned north toward San Antonio, got out a burner phone, and called Rawlings.

"Where you calling from?"

"Burner."

"What's up?"

"Two suits came to my house asking questions about San Mateo. When I left, they were following me, so I ditched them."

"What kind of questions?"

"Was I there last week. What do I do for a living. Am I traveling anywhere."

"So you jumped the gun. They didn't know anything."

"They knew I'd been to San Mateo."

"So what? You must have been on a surveillance camera near the nursing home. If they had any evidence, they would have arrested you."

"You want me to go back?"

"Not now. Now you look guilty as hell. You'd have to admit to something to explain why you rabbited."

"Bad attitude? Behind on my child support?"

"No. You need to go away for a while, but I need you where I can find you. Can you meet me in Oklahoma City?"

"I can get there."

"Three days. I'll have IDs and cash."

"Thanks, Major."

"Stay out of sight."

KD AND BLUNT stopped for dinner at Ricky's Barbeque in San Antonio. It was a cavernous, sheet metal building where the walls were covered with cowboy kitsch—saddles, ropes, old posters, animal hides. The food was excellent. After KD rubbed her hands with a wet wipe, she dabbed her mouth with a napkin. "I'll admit it. You were right."

"Some places claim they have barbeque, and some places have barbeque," Blunt replied.

"But I get to choose next time."

"No vegan joints."

She rolled her eyes. "Let's go over what we know."

"We know the nerve agent was released at the nursing home in San Mateo," Blunt replied.

"We know O'Malley was there, and we know he's done something."

"But we don't know what."

"He could have been on some other job," KD said.

"Could be. But why lie about being there? He had to know we knew he was there."

"His military record looks good. Five tours before he went into the private sector."

"And Accelerated Results Associates has a clean record. Looks like Major Howard Rawlings runs a tight ship. All those redacted pages only mean one thing."

"A lot of classified work."

"But that's been drying up lately. Still a lot of convoy protection and gate guarding, but that's not going to interest guys like O'Malley," Blunt said.

"Speaking from experience?"

"That's how I ended up getting up to stupid."

"What did you do?"

"We having a come-to-Jesus meeting?"

"Say or don't say. It's up to you."

Blunt shrugged. "Some guys robbed a bank owned by an Afghani warlord. I was supposed to help them get the money out of the country."

"Bank robbery?"

"Hell, it was US money that the warlord skimmed. We deserved it more than he did."

"But you got caught?"

"The guys got busted before I was to do my part. I thought I was in the clear, but somebody ratted me out. Can't blame them. Anyway, I lied and denied. Stuck to my story. But after that, my career stalled. All the officers I reported to were looking at me like I was dirty, couldn't be trusted. I started looking for a landing spot. Garcia reached out. I promised never again. End of story."

"So here we are."

"Here we are. Trying to earn our pay. Think Rawlings will tell us anything useful?"

"I don't know. His military record is squeaky clean. So your guess is as good as mine."

The next morning, KD and Blunt were sitting at the table in KD's motel room drinking coffee. They were packed and ready to go back to the airport. KD input the number for Accelerated Results Associates into her smartphone and put the phone on speaker.

"Accelerated Results Associates, Rawlings here."

"Major Rawlings, I'm Agent Thorne with the National Defense Agency. I've got you on speaker with my partner, Agent Blunt."

"I understand that you want info about one of my guys?"

"Bill O'Malley."

"Can you tell me why?"

"No, sir, I can't."

"You know how personnel files are. I can't just give out information on your say-so."

Blunt cut in. "Might be hard to get a new contract with this file open. As competitive as things are right now. Just saying."

"Are we talking national security?" Rawlings asked.

"Yes, sir," KD replied. "Any help would be appreciated."

"Off the record?"

"Off the record."

"Okay, I'll pull up his file." There was a pause on the line. "He came on with us straight out of the army four years ago. He's got a clean record, done good work in the field. I'm not really sure what you're looking for."

"He's never been involved in any questionable activities?"

"Not that we're aware of."

"Does he have more than one home? A hunting or fishing place?"

"Not that I know of."

"What about family?"

"He's divorced. No kids, I think."

"Where is she at?

"I have no idea. That was before he separated from the army."

"Major Rawlings, how many employees do you have?"

"When I have a full contingent? Eight."

"That's all?"

"We're a specialty operation. I assume you've pulled our file. We're an extraction team. We do kidnaps, ransom recovery, document acquisition. We're a tight crew."

"But you don't know anything personal about Mr. O'Malley?"

"A team functions better if you keep everything professional."

"I understand. If he gets in touch, would you contact me at this number?"

"Absolutely."

"Thank you for your time." KD ended the call.

"That guy's more convincing than O'Malley, but he's still lying about something," Blunt said.

"Yeah, a crew that small, everyone knows everything about each other." She slipped her phone back into her pocket. "Let's get back to DC and figure out how we can turn him into a lead."

Two days later, Rawlings flew into Dallas/Fort Worth using a fake ID, picked up a rental car, and drove to Oklahoma City, where he checked into the Fairfield Inn and Suites downtown. He was lying on the bed watching a news channel when his burner phone rang.

"Yeah?"

"Major, it's O'Malley. Have you got my gear?"

"There's a gentleman's club south of town. Busty's. Meet me in the parking lot at ten o'clock."

He ended the call and went into the bathroom to splash water on his face. What a mess. The Feds digging into their business. O'Malley shooting from the hip instead of thinking on his feet. At least he'd managed to get here without getting caught. Rawlings dried his face on a hand towel. He needed to make sure there were no mistakes tonight. Everything needed to go just right if they were going to get the Feds off their backs.

At 9:30, Rawlings was sitting in a stolen Ford Ranger in the back corner of the Busty's parking lot between the side of the building and a parked semitruck. Busty's had seen better days. The comments on Yelp were mostly negative—beer too expensive and dancers who tried to cheat you—and the parking lot was still mainly empty, even if country music was blaring out of the front of the building and the stereotypic, muscled-up bouncer stood at the door. Rawlings was parked facing out, where he could watch the traffic in the parking lot. The cops crawled by at 9:45. The bouncer waved. A few regulars parked close to the building and went inside.

Exactly at 10:00, O'Malley pulled into the lot, still driving his Jeep Wrangler. Rawlings shook his head. No initiative. He was beginning to wonder how O'Malley had managed to stay alive this long. Rawlings flashed his lights. O'Malley backed in beside him and climbed in the passenger's side of the Ford.

"Hey, Major."

"Long drive?"

"Not too bad."

"Where did you stop?"

"Slept in the Jeep."

"Your package is in the glovebox. Driver's license has the same picture as your current one."

"Great. Where do you want me to wait?"

"Go to Denver. Take this truck. It's got clean plates. I'll dump the Jeep."

"Right now? Thought I might have a look inside the club."

"Right now. You can't be seen in this town."

"Okay, let me get my gear."

They both got out of the truck, Rawlings following O'Malley around to the driver's side of the Jeep.

"Keys?" Rawlings asked.

"In the ignition."

O'Malley opened the back seat door and reached in for his bag. Rawlings snapped open a lockback knife, dove onto O'Malley's back, pushing O'Malley's face into the seat and stabbing him in the kidney as they went down, and then reached up and cut his throat as he struggled to get free. He glanced out into the parking lot. All clear. He rolled O'Malley off the back seat onto the floorboard and shut the door. Then he went back to the Ford, wiped down the front seats where they'd been sitting, locked the truck, and tossed the keys underneath. There was no escape package.

He got into the Jeep and waited, watching the parking lot. He hated having to kill O'Malley, but he didn't have any choice. Dead kid. Feds on their backs. He couldn't let anything affect this payday. He'd finally gotten things straightened out with Julie, and the guys were counting on him. O'Malley had only himself to blame. Getting caught on camera in San Mateo. Going back to his own house afterward, without making sure he was in the clear. If the authorities captured him, he'd have talked for sure. The rest of them couldn't chance that. He chose O'Malley for the San Mateo job. It was his responsibility to make sure everyone else on the team was safe.

A Camry pulled into the parking lot. Three men got out. Rawlings gave them a minute to get to the door. While the bouncer was busy with them, he started the Jeep and drove out of the parking lot. This was the most dangerous time. Get stopped by the cops, and it would be a shootout or prison for sure. No way he'd slip by. The smell of blood and shit was already wafting up from the back floorboard. He drove just below the speed limit, used his turn signals like he was taking the driver's test, and took the shortest route to the interstate. Two exits down, he got off and pulled into an out-of-business diner with a shattered parking lot sign and plywood nailed over the windows. His rental car was parked behind the building, just where he'd left it.

He parked the Jeep on the broken asphalt about ten feet from the building, went to his rental car, popped the trunk lid, and took out a five gallon can of gas. This was the best way to protect everyone. Rawlings poured the gasoline over the front seat and over O'Malley in the back, tossed the gas can into the Jeep and lit a match. He watched the fire catch on the seats before he jogged over to his rental car and drove away. Did O'Malley have a kid? He told the federal agents no, but he couldn't remember. He remembered O'Malley's ex was always bitching about something—gambling, unpaid bills, drinking. O'Malley just wasn't cut out for civilian life. If there was a kid, when this was all over and they were all back on their feet, maybe he'd put some money in a college fund to help the kid out.

He drove back to his motel, parked in the lot, and went across the street to Jimmy's All-Stars. The place was half-empty. He sat at the end of the dark wood bar that was farthest from the baseball playing on the TV. It was late in the east, but he called Julie anyway. Things were better between them, but they were still in a fragile place.

"Hey, baby," she said.

"Hey. Is this too late?"

"I was still reading. How was your day?"

"I'd hoped to line up a new job today, but it didn't work out. I'll be home tomorrow. I still have that payday coming I told you about, though, so fingers crossed. How was your day?"

"Showed a few houses. Needed financing to close a house, so I gave Raul the bad news."

"How did he take it?"

"We were in a Caffeination, so he stammered, turned red, told me to drop dead. I shrugged, reminded him how much he loved his family. I think we're good."

"And now he knows how it feels."

"I don't want to do this anymore than I have to."

"I get another job lined up and we'll be in the clear."

"I'm glad we got things sorted out."

"Me, too. I'll be home around three."

"I love you."

"I love you, too."

5

KD and Blunt were in their office, going through the unredacted files on Accelerated Results Associates, digging through Rawlings's life with a fine-tooth comb, looking for any info that might be of use in finding the nerve agent, when Blunt got a phone call from the FBI's Oklahoma field office that O'Malley's body had been found.

"What are the details?" KD asked.

"Highway Patrol found him in a burned-out Jeep behind an abandoned building on a country road just off the interstate."

"How can they be sure it's him?"

"Jeep was his. They matched his DNA from his service record."

"Lucky the fire didn't obliterate all the evidence. What was he doing in Oklahoma?"

"Who knows? But now we know for sure he was dirty," Blunt said.

"But that doesn't mean he was involved with the nerve agent release. Him being in San Mateo could still be coincidence."

"Either way, Rawlings is our only lead now."

"We need to put him under surveillance. Do you think we have enough evidence for a court order?"

"We don't need a court order. We don't arrest bad guys and charge them with crimes. That's somebody else's job. We just need the okay from Garcia."

MEANWHILE, Allen McCuller stood at Martin Jacobs's front door, a green duffel over his shoulder. Jacobs looked past him out to the street. "You sure you weren't followed?"

"Positive. I looped around twice."

"Come in."

Jacobs led him through the living room to the kitchen. "It's in the duffel?"

McCuller nodded. He set the duffel down on the kitchen table and unzipped it to show the canister of nerve agent. "Just as I promised."

"Wow," Jacobs said. "Is it safe to handle?"

"Completely safe. But you'll need to set up a clean room to work with it."

"We've got a guy to help us with that." Jacobs picked up the nerve agent canister and hefted it in his arms. "I have to admit that I didn't really think you would come through. We haven't created an operational plan yet."

"You don't want to take too long. The Feds are going to be looking for it. Besides, you don't need a serious plan to begin with. Just use a little, see what happens, then you'll be able to see what to do next."

"Maybe you're right," Jacobs said.

"If you need help with the technical end, I know a few people that might want to help."

"Thanks, but I think we can manage."

"Hoping to hear great things."

"You will. You definitely will."

Jacobs put the canister back into the duffel. "Thanks for doing this, Allen. You're a true patriot. I don't want to rush you off, but I need to move this stuff to a safe place." He shook McCuller's hand. "Will you be at the next meeting?"

"Absolutely."

"See you then."

McCuller drove away from Jacobs's house, circling around and taking a few extra turns to make sure he wasn't being followed. After he took the entrance ramp onto the freeway, he called James Dayton at BRK Pharmaceuticals. "It's done."

"Great. Exercise your stock options. You want to be all in when the run starts."

"I don't know. I don't have a lot of confidence that Jacobs is going to get things done anytime soon."

"What are you talking about?"

"We chose them because they're incompetent, remember? Well, according to Jacobs, they haven't done any planning yet."

"They need to act as soon as possible. If they wait too long, we'll already be fired. We're hanging on by a thread here. You're going to have to find a way to push them."

"They don't trust me that much."

"Why not? You're a stand-up guy. You gave them the nerve agent."

"Yeah, but from their point of view, I could be the FBI setting them up."

"When's their next meeting?"

"A couple of days."

"Tip the cops."

"They'll blame me for sure."

"So long as we can get them to act, who cares? After the cops harass them, they'll want to get a move on. They'll use the XP, they'll be arrested, they'll all go to jail. They won't be able to bother you."

"I don't know if it's a good idea to push them."

"We've got no time. Get it done."

THE NEXT AFTERNOON, KD and Blunt sat in a van on the street around the corner from Rawlings's house in the Maryland suburbs. They'd requisitioned a stingray device—a short-range cell phone tower simulator—and all the cell phone calls within a block of their location were being routed through the device. Any time Rawlings used his phone, or an unidentified phone was used from his house, the technician would isolate the call and record it. And when Rawlings's weather app had downloaded an update that morning, the technician had slipped in a trojan horse that cloned Rawlings's phone onto a tablet computer, as well as hijacking the phone speaker to listen in on any conversations within range of the phone, whether or not it was turned on.

The technician, a twenty-something in jeans and running shoes, looked up from his computer screen. "He's making a call on an unidentified phone."

"Pipe us in," Blunt replied.

The technician turned the speakers up.

"I had to deal with the guy who went to San Mateo," Rawlings said.

"I'm sorry about that," a man's voice replied. There were traffic noises in the background.

"Not as sorry as me. Why are you taking so long? When do you guys pull the trigger? My guys want to get paid."

"There are some variables involved that don't concern you. All I can say right now is that our timeline is solid. Everything is going to happen in the next couple of weeks. So just hang tight, the money will come streaming in, and you'll get your share. Don't call again. I'll be in touch when it's time."

The call ended.

"So Rawlings killed O'Malley," KD said.

"He's a brutal bastard," Blunt said. "But we still don't know if they were involved with the nerve agent or something else."

KD turned to the technician. "Anyone live there besides him and his wife?"

The technician shook his head. "Just them."

"So there's no small talk or planning sessions. Can we trace that last call?"

"Not long enough. And the trace would just take us to the closest cell tower to the phone."

"Which doesn't give us the caller," KD said.

"But we're collecting good intelligence," Blunt said. "Let's give it a few more days. See if we can find out what's really going on."

MCCULLER PULLED over on a side street near the BRK Pharmaceuticals building after he ended his call with Rawlings and called Dayton.

"So Rawlings is antsy," Dayton said.

"Had to kill his guy, wants to get paid and forget about the whole thing."

"What do you think we have to pay him?"

"He won't believe anything less than 200 K."

"That much?"

"He'll expect more. He's no fool. He'll watch the stock prices and estimate how much money was made."

"But he won't know how much stock I bought."

"He'll assume that you'll try to cheat him."

"Have you primed the pump?"

"I tipped the sheriff's department about dangerous fanatics planning terrorism, so they should be at tomorrow's meeting."

"Exercise your stock options. Borrow all the money you can. Buy all the BRK stock you can get your hands on."

"You think it will go that big?"

"We're going to be rich."

DAYTON ENDED THE CALL, drove into the garage of his house, and walked through to the kitchen. His wife, Brenda, an apron on over her dress, was cooking supper. Covered pans were on the stove, steam rising, and she was at the sink, her hands busy in the running water. He slipped up behind her, put his arms around her, and kissed her neck. "This is a great surprise. Smells good."

"Me or the food?"

"Both." He ran his hand along her hip.

She laughed. "You're in a good mood."

"Have you got wine open?"

"In the fridge."

He poured a glass of white wine.

She turned from the sink and laid out some lettuce on a kitchen towel to drain.

"Didn't expect you to be home," he said.

"My day off."

"And cooking."

"Just felt like it."

"I'm going to change."

He took off his suit, put on jeans and a sweater, and stopped in his home office to double check his stock purchases. Everything looked perfect. He went back to the kitchen. Brenda was standing at the cooktop, stirring a tomato sauce.

"You know, honey, it's been a tough six months for me."

"I know it."

"But now it's finally smooth sailing."

"Glad to hear it. You've been kind of cranky."

"I know it. I want to make it up to you. We should get away for a week or two. Go up to the cabin. Get the kids to come with us. Do the complete family R&R before the kids go back to school."

"A whole week? I don't know if I can get away that long. You know what the café's finances are like. I'd have to pay someone to take my place. And the kids have their jobs."

"I say we splurge. We deserve it. The summer's almost over. The kids can afford to miss a few days on their internships. We shouldn't miss an opportunity to all be together. Once the kids are out of college, it will be harder and harder."

"I don't know what's come over you, but okay, I'll talk to Ken. See who we can sub my hours to."

Dayton sipped his wine. Just in case, he thought. We'll be far away. If this project goes out of control—it's not going to happen, but if it does—his family will be safe. No use making the money if you're not around to spend it.

. . .

THE NEXT EVENING, after dark, Martin Jacobs and Marie Adamescu were sitting in a booth at the Travel Ace Truck Plaza restaurant at the east interchange into Franklin Ford, drinking coffee. The supper rush was long over. Waitresses were wiping tables and setting down napkin-wrapped utensils for the morning crowd. Jacobs held his coffee cup with both hands. "A friend in the sheriff's department called me."

Adamescu set her coffee down. "Let me guess. Anonymous tip."

He nodded.

"So I was right about Allen."

"He's definitely a liability."

"And he's not a cop. A cop would just roll up with a SWAT team and arrest everyone. Can you take care of him? I know you said you could, but if there's a problem, now's the time to tell me."

"He's no problem."

"Good. We're on his boss, so that's all the loose ends."

Jacobs looked at the bill and put some cash on the table. "You ready?"

They walked out into the parking lot where a semitruck sat idling. Two men in coveralls climbed out of the cab. Jacobs waved at a Ford Escape parked on the other side of the gas pumps. It flashed its lights before starting across the lot. After it parked next to the truck, a fat man with a pistol holstered on his hip got out. "Don't mind Lenny," Jacobs said, "he can be overdramatic. Let me show you what you got."

They walked over to the Escape. Jacobs opened the passenger door. The green duffel sat on the seat. He unzipped it to show the canister. "A friend of ours at a vet lab says this stuff is real."

"I know you wouldn't try to play us," Adamescu said. "But if it's not as advertised, we'll want our gear back."

"Of course."

"Let's take a look in the truck."

Adamescu's men opened the back of the semitruck trailer. One of them shined a flashlight inside. Gun and ammunition crates filled the back.

"All the gear off your list that we agreed to," she said. "M4 rifles and M17 Sig Sauer pistols. Not knockoffs. The real weapons your military uses."

Jacobs grinned. "We've been waiting a long time to get our hands on gear like this."

"The C-4 and blasting caps are at the other end if you want to climb in and look."

"I trust you."

"You can keep the trailer if you like," she replied, "but you need to lose the semi."

"I am so stoked," Jacobs said. "We're going to do great things."

Adamescu's men closed the back the of trailer.

"When will I see you again?" Jacobs asked.

"I'm always coming and going. And I like staying at your place."

"'Til next time, then."

"'Til next time."

They hugged and kissed.

"Come on, Lenny," Jacobs said.

They got into the semitruck, Lenny driving, and took the beltway north to an exit into an industrial area. They drove by a salvage yard, a sheet metal fabricator, and an auto body shop before they pulled up to the gate in a chain-link fence surrounding several rusted sheet metal buildings. "Your uncle never comes out here?" Jacobs asked.

"He's in a care center, Marty. And my cousins don't live here anymore."

Bell, dressed in gray coveralls, stepped out of the shadows and pulled open the gate.

Lenny drove into the compound and backed up to the loading dock of the building located furthest from the gate. Rob, a cap pulled down on his face, was standing by the open garage door. Lenny and Jacobs climbed out of the truck.

Jacobs hollered up at Rob. "Go get the forklift. Let's get this gear unloaded."

Ninety minutes later, all the crates were stacked in a locked storeroom in the warehouse. Jacobs, Lenny, Bell, and Rob were gathered on the loading dock. Jacobs padlocked the garage door. "Nobody gets to know about this. I chose you guys because I knew I could count on you."

"We're finally going to see some real action," Bell said.

"One step at a time," Jacobs replied. "We need the right target and the right plan." He turned to Lenny. "Get rid of the truck. We'll lock the gate behind you."

THREE DAYS LATER, McCuller sat on a barstool in a hotel bar in Wilmington, Delaware, sipping on a rum and Coke and watching the women. He knew that prostitutes worked this venue, and he was wound up, needed some physical contact that didn't require anything emotional from him. For the right girl, the right look, he was willing to pay. The last few days had been crazy. Jacobs had cancelled the club's meeting and hadn't returned his calls, Dayton had been whining about nothing happening, and Rawlings had called him from God knows where, demanding payment.

A blonde in a cocktail dress stepped up to the bar next to him, not too close, a clutch purse in her right hand, a diamond ring—maybe a good fake—on her finger, gave him a glance and a smile, and motioned toward the bartender.

"Yes, miss," the bartender said.

"Prosecco," the blonde replied.

McCuller watched her from the corner of his eye. Young, but not too young, meat in all the right places. Was she available or just in the wrong bar?

The bartender brought her Prosecco. "Starting a tab?"

"Put it on mine," McCuller said.

For a second, he thought she might say no, but she smiled instead. "Thanks." She shifted slightly toward him. "Unwinding?"

"It's been a long day of meetings. I go home tomorrow. So, yeah, I'm having a few. What about you?"

"I'm in here every now and again. It's safe, and the guys in here tend to be gentlemen."

"I'm glad to be included, then."

"We'll see." She smiled with her eyes. "I was wondering if we've got the same thing in mind."

"Maybe we do," he said.

"You're not wearing a wedding ring. You married?"

"No."

"Good. I hate to hear a guy talk about his wife all evening."

"All evening?"

"You got somewhere else to go?"

"I take it I'm paying for this good time?"

"Right to the point. With protection, one fifty buys a night of fun."

"Order me another round. I'll be back."

Simmons watched him disappear into the men's room. After the bartender brought his fresh drink, she slipped a vial out of her purse and poured some white powder into it. By the time McCuller finished that drink, he was slurring his words and swaying in his seat. Simmons glanced over her shoulder to Bell and Lenny, dressed in khakis and sportscoats and sitting at a corner table. They came over. "I'm so glad you're here," Simmons said to Bell. "Allen's overdone it again."

Bell and Lenny took McCuller under the arms and led him out of the hotel, his head lolling from side to side. Simmons held the door. "Where are you parked?"

"In the alley," Lenny said.

A few cars drove by, but there was no one on the street. In the alley, a Volvo sedan was parked next to a dumpster. "You sure that's his car?" she asked.

"Yep," Lenny replied.

She pulled open the driver's door. Bell and Lenny put McCuller in the driver's seat. Bell adjusted McCuller's feet into a natural position on the floorboard.

"Watch the alley," she said.

Lenny went to the far end of the alley, his hand on the pistol in his pocket. Bell went to the near end and stood on the sidewalk as if he were waiting for someone. Simmons got in the passenger side of the Volvo, pulled up McCuller's sleeve, and tied off his arm with a rubber strap. Then she took a syringe loaded with a heroin-fentanyl mixture from her purse and injected him. She left the syringe in his arm and loosened the strap. He appeared to stop breathing. She put two fingers on his neck to feel for a pulse. There was none. She locked the car doors and slammed her door shut after she got out.

She whistled at Lenny. Bell was already moving down the sidewalk to where they'd parked an old Toyota Previa van on the street. Lenny caught up to them just as Bell started the van. Simmons glanced back toward the hotel. A yellow cab stopped in front and a man and a woman got out and went into the hotel, chatting as they walked, but they didn't look up the street. As soon as Bell turned onto the freeway ramp, Simmons got out her phone. "All taken care of, Marty, just like you wanted."

"Thanks, Olivia. I knew I could count on you. You coming over?"

She turned toward the window and whispered. "We've talked about this. You're with Marie and I'm with Eric now. You missed your chance."

"Marie's not here anymore."

"But when does she come back? I won't be the side girl. See you tomorrow."

THE NEXT AFTERNOON, James Dayton was driving up a two-lane highway into the Allegheny mountains. He was meeting his wife and kids at their cabin. Limited internet, satellite TV, hiking, and simple, home-cooked meals. Exactly the antidote he needed for all the stress he was under. He hadn't been able to get in touch with Allen over the last twenty-four hours. Was that good or was that bad? Had Allen finally gotten back in with the Patriot Alliance idiots? Was he finally going to make something happen? If it didn't happen soon it wouldn't matter.

Up ahead, he saw a sheriff's cruiser on the side of the highway, its blue and red lights pulsing. A deputy was standing in the road directing traffic, while his partner was standing behind a utility van talking with three men in work clothes. Dayton slowed to a crawl as he approached. The deputy in the road held up his hand for Dayton to stop, and then came around to Dayton's window, his hand resting on the pistol holstered on his hip. Dayton lowered the window. "What's up, deputy?"

"Need to pull over, sir. Prisoner escape. We need to look in your trunk."

Dayton pulled over to the side of the road. The deputy followed. "Driver's license and registration."

Dayton took his license from his wallet and the registration from the glovebox. The deputy looked them over and handed them back. The other deputy continued to talk with the men behind the van. "Okay, step out of your vehicle and open the trunk. Then you'll be on your way."

"There's no one hiding there."

"I know. You still need to do it. When the sheriff asks me, I need to be able to tell him I looked in every trunk."

Dayton got out of his BMW, stepped around to the back, and used the fob to open the trunk. It was as empty and clean as when it came from the dealership. He turned to the deputy. "Anything else?"

The deputy smacked him across the face with his pistol. Dayton fell to his knees, his hands going to his bloody face. The three workers and the other deputy ran over. The deputies kept their eyes on the highway. Two of the workers held Dayton on his knees while the third one poured a pint of vodka down his throat. He sputtered and gagged. "What the hell?" he yelled.

The man hit him with the empty bottle. "Shut up."

The man drove Dayton's BMW to the edge of the right of way where the safety cable guarding the drop-off had been knocked down. The other two men dragged Dayton to the car and shoved him into the back seat, and then the deputies rushed over and all five of them pushed the BMW over the edge. The BMW shot straight down, then rolled end over end, broke through some pine trees, and crashed upside down on a boulder.

The first deputy took out a cell phone. "The loose end is tied off."

"Thanks for your help."

The men got into the utility van and the deputies got into their cruiser. They both U-turned and drove back down the mountain.

JACOBS, Olivia Simmons, Bell, and Lenny sat on lawn chairs around the firepit in Jacobs's backyard. They could hear children playing in a neighbor's yard and could smell meat cooking on a grill. "Just for the record," Lenny said, "I think this is a little paranoid."

"We've got the guns now," Jacobs said. "We can't afford to take any chances. McCuller ratted us to the sheriff, which could have turned out a lot differently if we didn't have friends there. The FBI could have the house bugged. If they do, all they know about is the Patriot Alliance business, not the Fatherland Volk work."

"Why aren't Rob and Cassie here?" Bell asked.

"I know they're friends of yours, but they're still too new to be in on planning."

"One step at a time," Lenny said. "That's the way we all came into the Volk. That's why nobody goes weak and turns on us."

"But they'll get their chance to prove out?" Bell asked.

"Absolutely," Jacobs said.

Simmons stood up and pushed a log farther into the fire with her foot. "So what's our first target? The turbans who own the falafel shop are still in town."

"Too close to home," Jacobs said. "We don't want the cops sniffing around here. It'll make our friends in the sheriff's department uneasy."

Lenny nodded. "So it's Philadelphia?"

Bell laughed. "I believe that's what they call a target-rich environment."

"We need to be careful around the historical buildings—Independence Hall, the Liberty Bell, that's all about white power," Simmons said.

"But there's a lot of illegals in Chinatown," Bell replied.

"And there's synagogues and mosques," Lenny said.

"Black Muslims," Simmons said.

"Easy to blend in around a synagogue," Bell said.

"You're right," Jacobs said. "Synagogues are in white neighborhoods. Easier to do recon, develop a plan to set a bomb."

"So we learn how to make and set bombs to blow up a synagogue —is that what you're saying?" Lenny asked.

"Exactly. Then we'll be ready to try a mosque or community center."

Simmons turned to Bell. "Don't you have a buddy who learned explosives in the army?"

"Yeah," Bell replied, "but he's got a black sister in-law."

"Can't we reach out to our Volk brothers and sisters?" Simmons continued. "That would be easiest, wouldn't it?"

Jacobs shook his head. "Cells coordinate action, but they have to stay operationally separate. That way the Feds can't infiltrate the entire organization."

"I know a guy who used to do mining demolition," Lenny said.

"Would he want to help?" Jacobs asks.

"Hates Mexicans. His ex married one."

"Feel him out."

"Okay."

"While we're getting our plan together, we need to do some live fire training," Jacobs continued. "Time for Rob and Cassie to move up from paintball."

"I just added on to the training course out at the farm," Lenny said. "There's a few more surprises down the hill near the creek."

Jacobs nodded. "So this is the plan. Lenny and I will scope out targets in Philadelphia, Lenny will reach out to his buddy about bomb making, and Eric and Olivia will start Rob and Cassie's gun training."

6

The next morning, KD and Blunt were sitting in their office reading through the last report from Agent Tina Han investigating the leads generated from the stingray at Rawlings's house. They had the transcript of a call with an individual referred to as "Allen," and that call traced to a cell tower near the home of Allen McCuller, a security consultant at BRK Pharmaceuticals who was found dead in an alley in downtown Wilmington, Delaware, the day before yesterday. The police report was attached.

KD laid her copy of the report down on her desk. "So McCuller OD'd. Tox screen indicates heroin, fentanyl, and ketamine.

"We're supposed to believe that a pharma security expert was shooting drugs in an alley? I don't buy it."

"Ketamine is a date rape drug."

"Which makes this look like a straight-up murder," Blunt said.

"Cops didn't find anything at his house." KD googled BRK Pharmaceuticals. The top item was a newspaper story about the death of James Dayton. "Get a look at this."

Blunt stepped up behind her and read her screen over her shoulder. "Dayton was the head of BRK's defense division."

"Hold on." KD paged through Tina's report. "McCuller consulted with that division."

"So McCuller's boss died in a car wreck yesterday, not even twenty-four hours after McCuller. No way this adds up."

"I wonder if Tina's got anything new for us."

Blunt called her. "Tina? It's Blunt and KD. We've got you on speaker. Just read your report on McCuller. Have you got an update?"

"McCuller was a loner. Frequented prostitutes. Couldn't find any drug history. That's about it. Or are you talking about Dayton? BRK is backpedaling pretty hard on that one. Dayton managed their defense division. It's being downsized. Gossip is that his behavior had become erratic, that he was going to be let go. They're worried he might be a suicide."

"Anything connect the two deaths?"

"Nothing. You want me to keep digging?"

"Yes. Look into their backgrounds and travel records."

"Will do."

Blunt ended the call. "Rawlings is in a bad place. On the transcript, he's demanding payment. He's not going to get paid now. Maybe we should put some pressure on him."

"See if he'll cooperate?"

"Exactly. He might need to start thinking about an exit strategy."

KD called the technician in the van outside Rawlings's house. "Is Rawlings at home?"

"Yes. He hasn't made any calls, but he's there. I can hear the at-home noises."

She ended the call. They drove out to the suburbs and parked on the street behind the surveillance van. Blunt phoned the technician. "We're going in."

They went up the steps to Rawlings's front door. KD pressed the buzzer. Rawlings came to the door in workout clothes. "Yeah?"

"Major Rawlings? I'm Agent Thorne and this is Agent Blunt. We spoke on the phone a few weeks ago."

"I remember."

"May we come in."

"I'm in the middle of something right now."

"Did you know that Allen McCuller is dead?" KD asked.

"He overdosed in a downtown alley in Wilmington, Delaware," Blunt continued. "That sound right to you?"

Rawlings leaned out his door and looked down the street both ways. "Come in."

They followed Rawlings down the hall to the living room. A painting of a field of wildflowers hung over the fireplace. Two leather sofas facing a round coffee table sat in the middle of the space. "Sit down."

KD and Blunt sat on one side, Rawlings on the other. "So McCuller is dead. What's that got to do with me?"

"You're not going to get paid, for starters," KD said. "You'll have to explain that to your crew."

Blunt continued. "Must be hard finding work with the wars winding down."

"I don't have the slightest idea what you're talking about."

"You know we're not cops, right? We don't have to follow cop rules. We're not arresting anyone. If somebody's done something bad enough, they end up wearing a head bag on their way to a black site. So cut the crap. We know O'Malley dispersed the nerve agent. And we know you killed him."

"That's not provable."

"You're not paying attention," Blunt said. "We don't have to prove anything."

KD continued. "We know you were pushing McCuller to get paid. Did you know McCuller's boss died yesterday? Horrible single car accident on a mountain road. Looks like alcohol was involved."

"So McCuller and his boss are dead?"

She nodded.

"Both of them?" Rawlings looked from KD to Blunt. "Anything I say is off the record."

"If that's how you want it."

"And you give me your word that you won't blackball me from getting contracts."

"If we get the truth."

Rawlings nodded. "McCuller hired me to obtain the nerve agent. He swore no one would get hurt, that it was just a business scam. There was supposed to be a big payoff. My end was going to be north of $200,000."

"And you blew up the storage facility?"

"That was to cover up taking the nerve agent."

"Why?"

"I don't know. McCuller kept everything compartmentalized. I only dealt with him, but I was under the impression that he reported up."

"But he used you to release the nerve agent?"

"Yeah. He said it was a test to see how the media would react, that he was sorry about the kid."

"And you sent O'Malley?"

"O'Malley was the only one of us who had access to a facility where people would receive immediate medical attention. We didn't want any fatalities. But sending him turned out to be a mistake."

"So you dealt with him?"

"What choice did I have? I had to protect the crew. He was the one who messed up. You two were after him. You saw how he was. He was swirling around the toilet. If was just a matter of time before he got caught and cut a deal that screwed the rest of us."

"What was McCuller planning to do with the nerve agent?"

"Don't know for sure. Since San Mateo was a test, I'm guessing some sort of contained release or threat of release. We weren't part of that."

"And how was that going to generate the kind of cash you were promised?"

"No idea."

"But you believed the money was going to be there?"

"He was convincing."

"So you gave the nerve agent to McCuller yourself?"

"Yeah."

"When was that?"

He looked at the calendar on his phone. "That was about six weeks ago."

"Where did he take it?"

"He didn't tell me, and I didn't ask."

"And then he came back to you with the aerosolized sample that O'Malley released at the nursing home?"

Rawlings nodded.

"When was that?"

"A few days before the release."

"That's everything?"

"That's it."

They all stood up.

"What a nightmare," Rawlings said. "I'm screwed without this payday. Me and my guys. But I guess it works out for you. Whatever they were planning isn't happening now."

"You aren't concerned that whoever killed them might be coming for you?" KD asked.

He shook his head. "I'm a professional soldier, not some wannabe in a suit and tie. Anyone comes for me will have a job to do."

"You think of anything else," Blunt said, "you give us a call."

KD and Blunt walked back out to their car. "That guy's a piece of work," KD said. "Murdered his own guy."

"For the good of the team." Blunt shook his head. "Sounded like he really believed it."

"But now we know who had the nerve agent."

Blunt nodded. "We need to find out who McCuller gave it to, or who took it from him."

"Are there any surveillance cameras in the area where he died?"

"Got to be at the hotel."

"Let's see what we can find out there."

Blunt called Tina to have her pull the surveillance camera feeds from the area around the hotel for the day before McCuller was found.

"She's on it."

.   .   .

LATE SATURDAY MORNING, Jacobs and Lenny were on Society Hill in Philadelphia, driving by a neighborhood synagogue. Families were streaming out the front entrance, stopping to talk with friends, the children rushing about on the sidewalk.

"Look at them," Jacobs said. "Masquerading as if they were human. So hard to spot when they're mixed in with white people. But when they're gathered together—" He pointed down the street. "Take the first right. Not this one. The next one."

"I hate these one-way streets," Lenny said.

"That's why we couldn't just look on google maps," Jacobs said. "We've got to know how to navigate down here."

"This is the third synagogue we can't just circle around."

"This is the city. Did you think we'd just drive up, throw the bomb, and drive away?"

"I wasn't thinking about it at all," Lenny said. "Looks like we'll have to plant the bomb ahead of time. Place it Friday night or early Saturday before services. We're going to need timers."

"Unless we jump out of a van all geared up, run in shooting, throw the bomb and run out."

"How would we time off the cops? And we'd have to plan the route to get clear of the one-ways and break for the freeway."

"I'm just brainstorming."

"Maybe Randy in the sheriff's office would know something."

"Randy will give us the heads-up or look the other way, but he's going to run in the other direction when it comes to direct action."

They passed by the front of the synagogue again.

"We done here?" Lenny asked.

"Drive back by the others one more time," Jacobs said. "I want to take a few more pictures."

ON MONDAY, KD and Blunt received an email from Tina Han with a knit-together video of the surveillance cameras on the streets surrounding the Wilmington hotel where McCuller was last seen alive.

They watched McCuller walk down the sidewalk and into the hotel. After a jump cut in the video, McCuller staggered out of the hotel, a man on either side of him and a blonde woman holding the door. The group moved down the sidewalk and into an alley. There was another jump cut. The men put him into the driver's seat of a Volvo. The woman got into the passenger's side. The two men moved to either end of the alley. A few minutes later, the woman got out of the car, there was a final jump cut back to the sidewalk, and she and the two men went down the street, got into a Toyota Previa van, and left.

"So they murdered him," KD said.

"We need to find those people."

"But does it have anything to do with our case? We don't know what those three were thinking. They could have roofied him to rob him, just got carried away with the drugs."

"They're our only leads," Blunt said.

"Give Tina a call."

Blunt called Tina and put his phone on speaker. "Tina, we've had a look at the video surveillance you sent us. That's some good work."

"Thanks."

"Could you dig into the databases to identify those three people and find that Toyota van?"

"I'll take care of it. Might take a couple of days."

Two days later, KD and Blunt were sitting at a table in a holding cell in the basement of the National Defense Agency building across from Olivia Simmons and Eric Bell. Simmons and Bell were dressed in orange jump suits and had their wrists cuffed behind their backs. Bell had a black eye. A laptop computer sat open on the table.

"Who the hell are you?" Bell asked. "And why did you bring us here?"

"You haven't read us our rights," Simmons said.

"Let's look at a movie," KD replied. She turned the laptop so that the screen faced Simmons and Bell and played the video surveillance. Simmons opened her mouth to speak but said nothing.

"You clean up real nice, Olivia," Blunt said. "And your boy here can pass for human with a sportscoat and khakis."

"You took McCuller into the alley and killed him," KD said.

"He propositioned me," Simmons replied. "So we rolled him. But he was alive when we left him."

"What do you think, Eric?" Blunt asked. "Do you think she'll be able to stick with that story all the way through the interrogation?"

"Go fuck yourself," Simmons replied.

"You two have a colorful history. Olivia, you've got a daughter who lives with your mother. Does social services know your mom's an alcoholic? She's already on the bottle at 10:00 a.m. And you're on parole, Eric, which means the guns in your basement are a strict no-no."

"You can't just dig through our lives," Bell said. "We've got rights."

"We can do whatever we want. And we will, until we find out what we want to know."

"Maybe the FBI would be interested in that club you two belong to," KD continued. "What's it called? Oh yeah. The Patriot Alliance."

Simmons leaned across the table. "What do you want?"

"Who sent you after McCuller?" KD asked.

"I told you, we were working the bar. Never saw him before. Rolled him."

"Let me show you another video." KD opened a new video. It showed a line of shackled prisoners wearing orange jump suits and head bags being loaded onto a military cargo plane.

"No rights, no lives," Blunt said.

"You can't do that," Bell said. "We're in America."

"Folks are always telling me that," Blunt said. "But the stuff happens anyway. One way ticket to the never-seen-again."

"We don't know anything about McCuller, but if we tell you something we do know, will you let us go?" Simmons asked.

"If it's important enough," Blunt replied.

Simmons turned to Bell. "Tell them about the truck."

"Are you crazy?"

"Okay, then, I will. Eric saw a semi loaded with weapons."

"Did you see the truck?" Blunt asked.

"No, but Eric did."

"Full of weapons?"

Bell nodded. "Military hardware. Cases of it."

"Where did it come from?"

He shrugged. "Picked it up at a truck stop. Drove it to a place on the highway. Came back the next day. It was empty. Drove the empty truck to another truck stop."

"Which one?"

"Truckers Mart."

"When was this?"

"About a week ago."

"Can we go?" Simmons asked.

"We'll see."

KD and Blunt walked down the hallway and into an empty office, where they called Garcia. "You're on speaker, boss," KD said.

"What's up?"

They filled her in.

"Patriot Alliance? I'm not familiar with them. Let me check the files." The line was quiet for a minute. "This doesn't make sense. They're just a lot of militia wannabes holding meetings and playing paintball in the woods. We don't have them connected to any criminal activity."

"Maybe they're finally stepping up," Blunt said.

"This is the only lead we've got," KD said. "The trail dead-ends with McCuller."

"Rawlings isn't holding anything back?" Garcia asked.

"We could always sweat him," Blunt said. "But I don't think his story is going to change."

"You really think these two are telling the truth about the guns?"

"It's the only thing they said that I believe," KD replied.

"Who's the Patriot Alliance cell leader?"

"Martin Jacobs."

They could hear her typing. "Lives in Franklin Ford, PA?"

"That's him."

"I'll authorize drone surveillance. See if it leads us to a weapons cache. Maybe it's connected to the nerve agent. In the meantime, you two need to dig deeper into McCuller. He gave the nerve agent to someone."

"The two we've got," KD said. "Hold them or turn them loose?"

"They're not going to tell Jacobs that they told us about the weapons. Tag them. Maybe they'll lead somewhere. After we're done with them, we'll turn them over to the police for the murder. Anything else?"

"What do you want to do about Rawlings?" Blunt asked.

"He doesn't have to worry about being blackballed because he's going to prison," Garcia replied.

"There's no physical evidence that he did any of the things he told us about—not the thefts or the murder," KD said.

"But he's desperate for work?" Garcia asked.

"Yeah."

"Then we'll use that," Garcia replied. "But he's not your problem. The nerve agent is. Get me some answers."

MEANWHILE, Marie Adamescu sat in the lobby of the administrative building at a private airfield in New Jersey. She wore a skirt suit with a colorful scarf draped around her neck. Two pieces of luggage sat on the floor beside her: an oversize, hardcase roller bag and the green duffel that contained the nerve agent. She was waiting for the plane that would take her to Spain.

A man came through the door from the tarmac wearing a navy-colored pilot's uniform and a captain's hat. "Ms. Adamescu?"

She stood up.

"Is this all your luggage?"

"The duffel stays with me."

The pilot turned to the woman working behind the counter. "Could you have the roller bag put on plane, please?"

"Yes, sir," she replied.

He turned back to Adamescu. "Can I help you with the duffel?"

"Thank you."

He shouldered the duffel. They walked out across the tarmac to the private jet that had its stairs down. When they were out of earshot of the building, the pilot asked, "Is this the bag that doesn't go through customs?"

"Yes."

"You'll get it back after you've rented your car. Your flight attendant uniform is hanging in the bathroom."

Once on the plane, Marie sat in a leather recliner and looked through the handbag that had been left for her. New ID, passport, and credit cards. She took out her burner phone and called the saved number. "I'm on the plane. I'll contact you when I reach Madrid."

SIMMONS AND BELL were down in the metro in Washington, DC, standing away from the other passengers, waiting for a metro car to take them to the Amtrak connection at Union Station. "Are we being followed?" she asked.

Bell glanced around. All he saw were suits heading home after work. "No—I don't know—how the hell would I know?" He pushed her into the shadows and put his hands on her hips to keep her close. "We going to tell Marty?"

"Yes."

"You sure that's safe?"

"Think it through. We told them about a truck that was dumped a week ago. It's not there anymore. Whoever reported it stolen is looking for it. If they find it, maybe there's some sort of residue from the weapons, but who cares? It won't tell them anything."

"Marty might think we're weak, can't be trusted."

"Marty knows he can count on us. Who else could he have sent after Allen? We did that job just right. And we're still free."

"Those Feds didn't have any trouble finding us."

"And they didn't keep us." She kissed him. "Marty needs us. We're the vanguard. When the action starts, who do you think's going to drive the explosives or lead the newbies?"

He let go of her and turned toward the tracks. "Assholes dumped us out here. At least they could have taken us to Philly."

"Just fucking with us. Showing they're in control."

"Wait til we get our chance. They'll find out who's fucking with who. Blow up their building just to watch them run outside."

She squeezed his hand. "You got that right. It's going to be our turn. We'll show them what patriots are."

BLUNT WAS on the phone with Tina Han. "GPS trackers working?"

"They're in the metro."

"Don't lose them."

"We've got trackers in their jackets and their shoes. Wherever they go, we go."

THE NEXT DAY, KD and Blunt were in the office, searching for any evidence of McCuller's movements over the last three months. Tech support was unable to get into his bank records or credit card records, but the GPS navigation computer on his car showed his driving patterns. After they cut through the static—grocery store, gas station, fitness center—they found weekly trips from Delaware into the Philadelphia area.

"Think maybe McCuller was visiting Jacobs?" KD asked.

"Let's find out." Blunt got on the phone with Tina. "What are the GPS coordinates of Jacobs's house?"

"I'll text them to you."

"Thanks."

Blunt turned to KD. "Looks like McCuller was driving up to Jacobs's for the Patriot Alliance meetings."

"So is that the connection we've been looking for? Did McCuller give the nerve agent to the Patriot Alliance? Did they kill him to cover it up? Let's take a road trip and get the lay of the land."

They drove up to Pennsylvania, fighting traffic on Interstate 95 as they left the Washington, DC, metro area. But after they got on the other side of Baltimore, they made good time until they closed in on Philadelphia, where they took Interstate 476 north around the west of the city and on up into Buckwall County. Traffic began to thin after they passed the last exit into Philadelphia. After they got off the interstate at the first interchange into Franklin Ford, they checked into a Holiday Inn Express, getting two rooms side by side.

While KD was putting her shower kit in the bathroom, Blunt knocked on her door. "Just heard from Tina. The drone followed Jacobs out to an old industrial warehouse at the north end of town. Business has been closed for years."

"Let's go out there after dark."

They took the interstate to skirt the west side of Franklin Ford and exited into an old industrial area. They passed a salvage yard and a sheet-metal fabricator, both closed and gated, before they came to a group of derelict warehouses surrounded by a chain-link fence that matched the GPS coordinates from the drone.

"I counted three buildings," Blunt said.

"Me, too."

"Padlock and chain on the gate look new."

"Front is too exposed," KD said. "Maybe we can get in the back."

Blunt took the next right, drove down a block past a heating and air-conditioning contractor, and took another right. At the end of the next block, they were behind the warehouses. The streetlights were spaced far apart. The only cars in sight were parked in front of a closed recycling center on the street behind them. Blunt pulled over next to the fence at a spot between the streetlights where the razor wire had rusted and fallen askew. They got out of the car and glanced around. Nobody was on the street. All they could hear were crickets and distant highway noise. Blunt opened the trunk and got out a mover's blanket, which he tossed over the tumbled down razor wire.

KD scrambled over and dropped down on the other side. Once on the ground she pulled her pistol and checked it. Locked and loaded. Blunt clambered over and dropped down beside her. Volunteer shrubs and saplings grew up in patches out of the weeds and blown-in trash. They made their way to the nearest building, staying low and moving fast. They looked in the back window. All dark. Blunt took out a penlight and shined it in. Stripped-down machinery. Disarray. No one had been in this building in some time.

They moved on to the next building, which was in the back corner of the lot. They climbed up the stairs to an emergency exit. All dark. Blunt shined the penlight in. Aisles cleared. Blunt took a set of lock picks out of his wallet, inserted the tension wrench into the bottom of the keyhole, pushed the pick into the top of the keyhole, and scrubbed it back and forth until the tension gave on the wrench and the bolt slid open. KD peered out into the gloom behind them. No one. Blunt slowly opened the door. No alarm. They slipped into the back of the warehouse and moved toward the front, illuminating their way with their penlights.

"Somebody's been here recently," Blunt said.

"Lots of tracks in the dust."

At the front of the warehouse, they found a forklift and a circle of lawn chairs in front of the garage-style door.

"Meetings?" Blunt asked. "Or something else?"

KD shined her light back into the room. "Storeroom on the left."

They walked back to the storeroom. It was padlocked. Blunt got out his lock picks. In a few minutes he had the lock open. KD pulled open the door. The room was stacked with crates of rifles and ammunition.

"Jesus," she said. "Look at the labels. This is all military."

"Still in the original cases," Blunt replied.

"This is a win, for sure," KD said, "but is it connected to McCuller? Did he give the nerve agent to Jacobs? Did Jacobs trade or sell it to get these weapons? Or is this just serendipity? We still don't know what we don't know."

"We know our info about the Patriot Alliance is bullshit," Blunt replied.

"That's for sure. Let's get out of here."

They locked the storeroom and the back door and made their

way back across the property to their car. While they were driving back to their motel, KD phoned Garcia.

Garcia sounded groggy. "What have you got?"

"We found the weapons cache at a warehouse up in Franklin Ford. Crates of rifles and ammunition."

"Send the location. I'll have the drone moved from Jacobs to cover it and coordinate with the ATF. They'll take over from here."

"Should we question Bell and Simmons again?"

"No, we don't want to spook them. Stay focused on Jacobs."

JACOBS, Simmons, and Bell sat around the fire pit in Jacobs's backyard. Lenny stood back by the gate in the fence, his pistol strapped on his hip. There was no fire tonight, the sky was overcast, and the neighbor dog was barking at something through the back fence.

Jacobs took a swig of beer and put the bottle down beside his lawn chair. "Let's go over what happened. You stuck to the story that you were rolling Allen, that you didn't know him, he was a perv, you gave him a taste of his own."

"That's it," Simmons said.

"You admitted to robbing him, and they didn't arrest you?"

"They're not cops," Bell said.

"That's what they said? Then what are they?" Jacobs asked.

"I don't know. Government agents. National Defense Agency? Nothing I ever heard of before."

"But they wanted to know about Allen?"

"Threatened us with rendition."

"But you didn't crack?"

They shook their heads.

"So what did you give them?"

"We were under pressure, Marty," Simmons said. "We didn't have any chance to get our story straight."

Bell continued. "It had to be something that seemed important."

Jacobs looked from one to the other. "So you told them ... ?"

"Olivia told them about the semi full of guns."

Jacob turned to Simmons. "You told them about our guns?"

"Just listen, Marty," Simmons said. "Lenny dumped that truck a week ago. There's no way they could find it. Plus it's empty."

"It's a wild goose chase," Bell said. "We didn't give any names. We said we just knew about the truck."

Jacobs shook his head. "I'd believe this story if you two were in jail. But you're not. Those Feds have to believe they're going to get more from you."

"That's all we told them," Simmons said.

"Then why are you here?"

"They dumped us out," Bell said. "Made us find our own way home."

"And they said they weren't cops?"

Simmons and Bell nodded.

"They had you in a lockup in DC? Picked you up at work?"

They nodded.

"Did they take your clothes away?"

"Yeah," Bell said. "Put us in prison clothes. Thought they could scare us."

"But they gave you your clothes back?"

"Yeah."

"Where have you been since you got back?"

"We went home. Stopped for some MacDonald's along the way. Went to work today. Came here."

"Oh, Christ," Simmons said. "You think they put trackers on our clothes?"

"How else could they hope to find the gear?"

"These clothes are fresh," Simmons said.

"Me, too," Bell said.

"What about your shoes?"

Bell looked at his feet. "I'm sorry, Marty. These are my work boots. We came here straight after work."

"But you haven't been to any of our other places?"

He shook his head. "I'll get rid of them."

Jacobs finished his beer. He had his hand on the revolver in his jacket pocket. "You two have anything else to say?"

"You know we're loyal, Marty. We've been with you from the beginning. You know we'd never do anything to put the group at risk," Simmons said.

"It sounds stupid now," Bell said. "But right then, telling them about the truck was the smartest thing we could do."

"What are you going to do, Marty?" Simmons asked. "You aren't going to cut us out, are you?"

"No, I'm not going to cut you out. You two get out of here." He looked at Bell. "And you keep wearing those boots. You just won't go anywhere that matters. Lenny will take you home. I've got some thinking to do."

Jacobs watched them leave through the gate in the fence. Soldiers, not officers. No imagination under pressure. That was disappointing. He looked out across the yard to the back fence. Federal agents, not cops, sniffing around what happened to Allen. This could turn into a problem. They needed to move the guns ASAP. Where to? Lenny's uncle's had been perfect until it wasn't. Couldn't be any place that was connected to any of them. But it had to be a place that they could control. What about his grandma's cabin out by the lake? Her name wasn't Jacobs. None of the family went out there anymore. The converted barn was big enough to store the speedboat, so the weapons would be an easy fit. It was a little too far out, and they couldn't leave the gear there forever, but for a week or two until he found somewhere better, it would work for that. They needed a permanent spot. But where? Didn't want to keep moving the gear. When they hit the first synagogue, the gear had to be in a place where they could get to it in a hurry but it couldn't be found.

7

In the morning, on the drive back down to Washington, DC, Blunt called Tina. "Thanks for the heads up yesterday. We're on our way back to the office now. Have you got anything new for us?"

"Before the drone was moved to the warehouse, it showed a gathering in Jacobs's yard last night. Couldn't see much in the dark, but Bell's tracker was there, so we're assuming two of the people were Bell and Simmons."

"We need for you to dig into Martin Jacobs. Phone records, emails, public surveillance footage, GPS, everything. We need to know all of his secrets."

"I'm on it."

Twenty-four hours later, Tina's report on Jacobs was in KD's and Blunt's encrypted email.

"So," Blunt said, "Jacobs is holding Patriot Alliance meetings at his house. That's where McCuller made contact. Something McCuller did, or promised, or didn't do, made him a risk. Jacobs had him killed."

"Not currently provable," KD replied.

"No, all we can prove is that Simmons and Bell killed him. And Dayton is even less provable. Particularly since none of the Patriot Alliance people seem to be involved."

"But we know McCuller had the nerve agent. And we know the Patriot Alliance took delivery of a weapons cache. What else do we know?"

"Except for his job, everyone Jacobs is connected with is Patriot Alliance," Blunt replied.

"Not the blonde woman, the one who's not Simmons. She's never where the rest of them are. Who is she? He's not married, so he's not having an affair. Why are they sneaking around?"

Blunt studied a grainy picture of Jacobs and a casually dressed woman sitting at a restaurant. "They're definitely friendly. Maybe Tina can dig up something more."

KD got a phone call from Garcia. She put it on speaker.

"The drone surveillance shows that crates were taken from the warehouse and moved out of Franklin Ford last night."

"All of them?" Blunt asked.

"We don't know."

"Isn't that the ATF's problem?" KD asked.

"It'll be our problem if the Patriot Alliance goes operational before the ATF gets up to speed. I'm sending you the details and the drone data. Get back up to Franklin Ford and find out what's going on. I'll get in touch with my ATF contact."

KD and Blunt drove back out to the dilapidated warehouses in the industrial area on the north end of Franklin Ford. A row of work vans was parked in front of the sheet metal fabricator and heavy equipment noises reverberated from somewhere within the salvage yard. Too many eyes to slip around to the back and climb the fence. KD drove up to the chain-link gate and Blunt hopped out to pick the padlock. Then they drove down the gravel driveway to the warehouse where they had found the weapons. Blunt picked the door lock. In daylight, the space seemed smaller and even more run down than it had in the dark. The forklift was now facing the garage-style door, and the lawn chairs were gone. They made their way back to the storeroom where the weapons had been stacked. The door hung open and the room was empty.

"They moved everything," KD said. She glanced around the rest of the empty warehouse.

"So they probably aren't going operational," Blunt said.

"No, looks like they got worried about their gear," KD replied. "They got tipped off somehow, or they're paranoid."

"Well, we rousted two of their people. Good thing the drone's hovering over the cache."

They got back in their car, KD driving. Blunt closed and locked the chain-link gate before they drove away.

"What's the drone's location?" KD asked.

Blunt looked at the map app on his phone. "A place called Mystery Lake. Get back on the interstate and head north."

They turned off the main highway onto the narrow gravel road that ran up to the private road that circled Mystery Lake. Thick woods and dense brush came up to the edges of the road on both sides. "What can you see?" KD asked.

"I've lost the internet. Cell reception is crap."

"So the drone's of no use?"

"Not from down here," Blunt said.

"You remember where the location is?"

"Yeah, we go to the right when we reach the loop around the lake."

"How do you want to do this?"

"Pull off the road by a hiking trail like we're just here for the day. Then we'll slip up on the property we're looking for."

When they reached the circle drive around Mystery Lake, KD pulled off at a wide place in the road. They got out of the car and made their way through the woods, moving quietly, taking their time, listening for dogs, cars, or voices, but they all they heard were birds and the wind moving through the trees. The first cabin they came to was locked down tight, plywood panels over the windows, as if the owners rarely came to the lake anymore. They stayed at the edge of the woods on the other side of the road and kept going. The second cabin had flowerboxes under the front windows and laundry hanging from a clothesline situated between the cabin and an oversize, two-car garage. The next cabin was the one they were looking for. It was larger—two story. The trees had been cut down behind it to give a view of the lake. A tarp-covered motorboat sat out in the yard on a concrete ramp that led down to the water. A Ford truck was parked beside it. Instead of a garage, there was a small red barn.

"So that's where the drone says the weapons are supposed to be," KD said.

"Wonder if anyone's home," Blunt replied.

Continuing along the tree line at the edge of the property, KD and Blunt made their way around to look behind the barn. Blunt touched KD's arm and pointed at the peak of the roof. "Surveillance camera."

They moved back toward the front of the barn, looking for other cameras, but that was the only one they saw. "We have to assume that camera is active," Blunt said. "We'll have to come at the barn from the side."

"But then we'll be seen from the house."

"If someone's there."

"Or there's another camera we haven't spotted."

Blunt looked at his watch. "About an hour until dusk. That would be the best time to avoid being seen."

They made themselves comfortable in the tall grass, watching the cabin and the barn, until the sun disappeared behind the lake. Then they ran across the road at a crouch, crawled across the open ground to the barn, and peeked in the small side window. The crates were piled on the far side of the barn. A skinny, bearded man sat in a lawn chair watching something on a tablet computer. Two cots and an old kitchen table completed the picture.

A door slammed.

KD and Blunt dashed back to the woods. A woman, mid-thirties, wearing jeans and a flannel shirt open over a T-shirt, carrying two plates of food, came out from the back of the cabin and walked across to the barn. After she went inside, KD and Blunt crept back across.

The man and woman were sitting at the kitchen table, eating. "At least it's peaceful out here," the woman said.

"Wish I'd brought my fishing gear," the man said.

"Maybe Marty will let us come out here for fun sometime."

"It's a beautiful spot. Reminds me of the cabin we stayed at on our honeymoon."

"Getting into the mood?"

"Don't tempt me. Marty's supposed to come by tonight."

"He said maybe."

"As worked up as he is, maybe means definitely."

KD and Blunt scurried back to the trees.

"So Jacobs is going to be here tonight," KD said.

"We've been lucky so far," Blunt replied. "Could have easily lost the weapons when they moved them. And we don't know if they're going to move them again."

"Or when they're going to start using them. Let's call Garcia, see what she wants to do."

It was full dark by the time KD and Blunt got back to their car. KD turned around and drove back out to the main highway where they could get cell reception. Then she called Garcia and put her on speaker phone. They filled her in.

"Watch for Jacobs in case he shows," Garcia said. "A couple of ATF agents I've liaised with before are on their way. It'll be their show."

KD parked on the shoulder of the main highway at a spot with a clear view of the turn onto the road leading to the lake. She turned off the headlights.

"Anything to drink in here?" Blunt asked.

"Bottle of water in the glove box."

"You saving it?"

"Go ahead."

He unscrewed the top on the water bottle and took a long pull. Then he passed it to her.

"Thanks," she said.

An old pickup truck drove by, traveling well below the speed limit, followed shortly by two shiny cars moving fast. Then a white Cadillac slowed down, turned on its blinker, and went down the road to Mystery Lake.

"That was Jacobs," Blunt said.

"You sure?"

"That's the Caddie from Tina's report."

A few minutes later, a sheriff's cruiser flipped on its red and blue lights and pulled over behind them. KD watched the cruiser in her mirror. Two deputies got out, one on each side, and moved up to their car, one deputy staying at the rear of their vehicle, while the other approached the driver's side window.

KD lowered the window.

The deputy shined his flashlight into the car. "What are you doing here sitting in the dark?"

"We're federal agents, deputy."

He shined his light on Blunt. "You two aren't from around here, are you?"

"My ID is in my jacket pocket," KD continued.

"Get out of the car and put your hands on the hood."

"We're federal agents, deputy. Can we show you our IDs?" KD asked.

"I told you to get out of the car and put your hands on the hood."

Blunt turned to KD. "No reason to argue, Doc." He swung his door open.

The other deputy pulled his sidearm. "Nice and easy, big fella."

Blunt slowly moved around to the front of the car and put his hands on the hood.

"Now you," the deputy outside the driver's side said.

KD pushed her door open and stepped around to the front of the car.

A black Ford Explorer pulled off on the other side of the highway. Two men wearing dark clothes and tactical gear climbed out and jogged across the road.

"What have you got?" the first men said to the deputy.

"They were already parked here when we arrived. Haven't had time to check them out."

The man turned to KD. "ID?"

She reached slowly into her jacket pocket and took out her National Defense Agency identification. The man looked at it and handed it back. "Glad you're here, Captain Thorne. I'm Glen Sloan, ATF." He turned to the deputy. "These are the people we were expecting, Scott."

Deputy Scott turned to KD. "Sorry about that, folks. We'd been briefed there might be lookouts posing as law enforcement."

Sloan turned to KD and Blunt. "What's the situation here?"

Blunt got out his smartphone to share the GPS information. "Best info is that there are three suspects with the weapons cache, which is located in the barn at the third property to the right—a man and a woman who've been babysitting, and Jacobs, who just arrived."

"This is the only road in?"

"Yes. It's dead quiet up there. I'm guessing most of the cabins are unoccupied."

A red Ford Focus put on its turn signal, slowed down, and turned up the road to the lake.

"Do you know that car?" Sloan asked.

"No," KD replied.

"SWAT team on the way?" Blunt asked.

"We're trying to keep this on the down low," Sloan replied.

"That makes six of us against maybe four, if the last car is one of them," KD said.

"Do they have tactical gear?"

"Don't know," KD replied.

"What they do have are enough weapons to fight a war," Blunt said.

"So we're going to have to be extra careful," Sloan said. "We've got body armor and rifles for you two."

"Warrant?" KD asked.

Sloan nodded. "All by the book."

"Then let's get this done," Blunt said.

KD and Blunt got in the Explorer with the ATF agents, the deputies following behind in their cruiser. They drove quickly down the rutted road in the dark, bouncing through the potholes.

"So the weapons are in the barn?" Sloan asked.

"The crates are stacked on the west side," KD replied. "The area around the cabin and barn is open. Once you reach the property there is no outside cover."

"What do you know about the people?"

"Jacobs doesn't have any military experience," KD said. "I don't know about the others."

"We'll park out of sight, work our way to the target through the trees."

At the cabin with the flowerboxes under the front windows, a spotlight lit the front of the house. The Explorer and the sheriff's cruiser pulled up into the yard. Sloan and Scott went up to the cabin and knocked on the door. An older woman pulled back the curtain on the closest window and peered out. Sloan held his ID up to the window. "ATF, ma'am. I'd like to speak to you."

The woman opened the door cradling a shotgun in one arm. "What do you want?"

"Ma'am, we're serving a warrant on your neighbor. We don't want you to be alarmed."

She nodded.

"Do you know them?"

"I know Dot, but she hasn't been out here for a long time. I'm thinking those are some of the grandkids and their friends."

"How long have they been out there?"

"Couple of days, I guess."

"We're going to leave our vehicles here, if you don't mind."

"Okay by me."

"Thank you, ma'am. You have a good evening."

KD and Blunt, the ATF agents, and the sheriff's deputies stood in the yard putting on body armor and checking their rifles in the light from the spotlight.

"Everyone ready?" Sloan glanced around the group. "Let's go."

The ATF agents took the lead, working their way along the tree line on the other side of the road until the two-story cabin and barn were in plain sight. Three vehicles were parked in the yard—the Ford Focus, the Cadillac, and the truck. The house was dark, but light shined out of the windows on the barn.

They stopped near the place in the brush where KD and Blunt had waited earlier. KD whispered to Sloan. "There's a surveillance camera at the back of the barn."

He nodded. "Was anyone in the house earlier?"

"The couple was using the house but staying in the barn to guard the weapons."

"So there's four people on the property."

"Must be."

"You and Blunt move down toward the back of the barn, we'll move in from here, the deputies will cover the road."

After everyone got into place, Sloan yelled down to the barn. "Mr. Jacobs. Federal agents. We have a warrant to search this property."

No answer.

He yelled again.

Blunt saw a glimmer at the back of the barn. He put a hand on KD's shoulder and pointed. Two people were moving across the open area, heading toward the lake. KD and Blunt ran at a crouch, moving as quietly as they could through the brush at the edge of the woods. The moon was shining off the water, putting the two figures in silhouette. A canoe sat on its side at the top of the beach. Blunt raised his rifle and placed two shots into the canoe. The figures shifted.

"Drop your weapons," KD yelled.

They heard a single shot behind them, followed by a hail of gunfire.

"Cease fire," Sloan yelled.

The silhouettes turned, hesitated. One of them took a step toward the water. "Last warning," KD said. "Hands up now."

Their hands went up. KD and Blunt, their rifles at their shoulders, moved toward the figures. It was Jacobs and a fat guy with an empty gun holster hanging from his hip. KD kept her rifle trained on them.

Blunt picked up their pistols and put them into his jacket pockets before he pulled Jacobs away, pushed him to his knees, and zip-tied his wrists behind his back. Then he zip-tied Jacobs's ankles together before he turned to the other man. As he zip-tied that man's wrists, they heard a woman screaming from the barn.

"Go on," Blunt said.

KD ran to the nearest window. The ATF agents and the sheriff's deputies were already inside. The woman she'd seen earlier was sitting in a folding chair at the kitchen table bawling. Her husband lay on the ground. The two deputies were rendering aid. KD opened the back door. "Sloan, we've got the other two."

He walked with her down to the lake, where Blunt was guarding Jacobs and his associate. "Let's get them up to the barn."

Blunt cut their ankle ties and pulled them to their feet. "Let's go."

Up at the barn, the injured man was in stable condition. "Cell reception is bad up here," one of the deputies said. "We'll have to radio for an ambulance from the cruiser."

KD took Sloan aside. "We need to get out of here."

"No need," Sloan said. "The warrant covers all of us."

"Garcia doesn't want the publicity."

"Okay," he replied. "I'll give you a lift back to your car."

They walked back down the road to the neighbor's house. The woman who lived there watched them from her window, but she didn't come outside. They put their body armor and rifles in the back of the Explorer, and Sloan drove them back out the narrow lane to the main highway.

"Enjoy the victory lap," Blunt said.

"Thanks for the help," Sloan said. "Tell Garcia I owe her one."

"She'll remember."

Sloan chuckled. "That's for sure."

The main highway was dark and quiet. KD and Blunt got back in their car, Blunt driving, made a U-turn, and drove back toward Franklin Ford. "That was sort of anticlimactic," KD said.

"Yeah," Blunt agreed. "It's not like a firefight, that's for sure. The shootout at the OK Corral is usually just boring unless some idiot misjudges the scene. And then it's the worst sort of clusterfuck—a pile of dead bodies with everyone pointing fingers and trying to dodge the blame. It's one of the things I really like about being one of Garcia's ghosts."

"No credit?"

"No responsibility. Besides, we don't have police powers, so we're easy to blame even if we've been 'deputized.'"

"We better bring Garcia up to speed." KD phoned Garcia and put her on speaker.

"So the entire shipment is out of circulation?" Garcia asked.

"Appears to be."

"ATF will be crowing tomorrow." Garcia paused. "But there're still no leads on the nerve agent?"

"No, boss," KD replied.

"I want your full report in the morning." She ended the call.

Blunt yawned. "What are we going to do next?"

"Get something to eat, spend the night at the Holiday Inn Express, make a fresh start tomorrow."

"I like the way you think."

8

On the drive back down to Washington, DC, the next morning, KD got a call from Tina. She put it on speaker. "Congratulations on getting Jacobs and the weapons."

"Thanks," KD replied. "But it was you and the drone that made the difference. What's up?"

"Your mystery lady was a hard nut to crack. Finally found her picture on a database of European rightwing extremists. She entered the US on a Romanian passport using the name Marie Adamescu, although I don't think she's actually Romanian."

"Thanks, Tina. Can you send what you've got?"

"Of course. I'll send an email right now."

When they got back to the National Defense Agency, they read the email. There was not much to go on. A headshot of a beautiful blonde with a sophisticated look. Date and time of her entry into the US. No indication that she'd left the country. Intelligence indicated that she was probably involved somehow in European rightwing terrorism, but that was it.

KD called Garcia and caught her up. "So the working theory," Garcia said, "is that Jacobs sold or traded the nerve agent to Adamescu?"

"Yes," KD replied. "She's the loose end."

"And that's how they got the weapons?"

"Had to be. We've got all of Jacobs's other contacts covered."

"It's a little thin."

"Maybe we can get Jacobs to flip."

"Okay, I'll talk to ATF. See if I can get you some time with him. I'll also get Adamescu's picture to Homeland in case she hasn't left the country and have the FBI issue an all-points bulletin. Our people can work on the international angle. If she has the nerve agent, we want to take her as quickly and quietly as possible. In the meantime, you keep digging."

THAT EVENING, Rawlings, Toms, Sebold, and Adler sat at a glass-topped table on the terrace of a seafood restaurant overlooking the Pacific Ocean. The waves were crashing against the rocks below and seagulls were flying over the beach gravel, looking for morsels. Their server had just collected their dinner plates.

"So we're screwed," Toms said.

"On the McCuller job? Definitely," Rawlings replied.

"That was a lot of days' pay," Sebold said.

"Tell me about it. I've got bills just like you. But there's no way to get paid out of this. This was an under-the-table job. We were in for a percentage. McCuller is dead. His boss is dead. The Feds are chasing the nerve agent."

"So we were fucked before we suited up on this job," Adler said.

"That's about the size of it," Rawlings replied. "I'd front you guys some cash to tide you over, but I'm just as broke as you."

"So what's next?" Toms asked.

"I'm hunting for work. I've lined up a personal protection detail for a visiting UAE sheik. We'll each pull down five thousand plus expenses."

"That won't even begin to dig me out of the hole," Sebold said. "The doghouse I'm in is all the way back at the property line."

"I'm working all my contacts. There might be a lot of short-term jobs until I line up a money-maker, but we're going to start getting paid."

"I'll go anywhere, Major," Sebold said.

"What about you other guys?"

"I don't want to spend six months lying in a ditch eating MREs, but if that's what it takes to catch up my mortgage—well, it is what it is," Toms said.

The other guys nodded in agreement.

"My wife told me to apply to the police or the fire department," Adler said. "Get a security guard job in the meantime. Just thinking about it makes me bored. You've got to come through, Major."

"My wife's no different, guys. She wants me earning. And that means anything but armed robbery. We do the sheik job at the end of next week; by the time we're done with that, I'll have something else lined up."

"What about O'Malley?" Toms asked. "Is he still not answering?"

"Like I said," Rawlings replied, "when he found out we weren't getting paid, he flipped out. I've called him, I've texted him. Nothing." Rawlings's mind flashed to O'Malley lying dead in the floorboard of the Jeep, but he kept a straight face.

"I tried calling him, too," Adler said.

"And he didn't pick up?" Toms asked.

Adler shook his head.

"He's a grown man," Rawlings said. "He gets to make his own decisions. But if he reaches out, he's back on the team if he wants in."

SHORTLY AFTER 11:00 P.M., KD stood in Frank's hotel room getting dressed in the light cast into the room from the bathroom.

"Sure you can't stay?" he asked.

"Early morning. Need to start the day from my place."

"We should have just gone there."

"Another time."

He sat up in bed. "Are you having as much fun as I am?"

"Where's this going?"

"Just want to know where we're at."

She sat on the edge of the bed. "When you're in town, I'm spending all my free time with you."

"And when I'm not in town?"

"There's no one else, Frank."

"You just seem a little distant at times."

"Yeah, well, things aren't the same as they were before, are they? If we're going to work out, we're going to find a new way to be the new us. That's just the way it's got to be for me."

He kissed her. "I appreciate your honesty. Want me to take you home?"

"No reason for you to get dressed. I'll be fine."

She took a rideshare from in front of the hotel. Was she actually ready to let Frank see her apartment? Being with him physically, sharing her feelings, seemed somehow safer than letting him into her place, even if it was a dumpy furnished rental. What was that about? Was it the last barrier that marked out the point of no return? When they'd moved in together senior year of college, it hadn't seemed like such a big deal. They were always either sleeping at her place or his place anyway. Just seemed like good economics. No, the first point of no return had been when he proposed. She'd been expecting it. She knew she'd say yes, but she still felt that queasiness like their relationship was finally all too real. The old queasiness.

"Pull over. I'll get out here."

"You sure?" the driver asked. "It's a couple more blocks."

"I want to walk."

The rideshare let her out at the corner. The neighborhood was peaceful. Only a few pedestrians were on the street. Top Forty music trickled out of the bar on the corner when the door opened and closed. A graybeard walking a Scottie nodded as he passed by her. She nodded back. She could see her apartment building at the end of the next block. She was going to have to make up her mind. They were completely intimate, but did she want to go back to being married? Or did she want to leave things as they were? Would he accept that? Over the short term, certainly. But over the long term?

How would she feel if she kept their relationship as it was now, and he came to her sometime in the future saying he'd found someone new? Someone who would be completely committed.

The blow to the back of her head knocked her into the wall of the building on her right. She pivoted and raised her hands, but not quite fast enough. The second punch caught her on the chin. Two guys swarmed in on her, showering her with body blows. Using one arm to shield her face, she pushed into the smaller guy, grabbed his crotch, squeezed hard and twisted. He shuffled back. She reached for the back of his head with her free hand, pulled him close, and bit his nose with all the force she could muster. He howled.

She spat blood and shifted toward the big guy. He swung hard for her eye. She bobbed, stomped on his foot, shouldered him toward the street, spun around as he grabbed at her jacket, and ran full out, crossing the street on the *Don't Walk* without checking for traffic. She looked over her shoulder half a block from her building. No one was chasing her, but she didn't stop running until she was digging her keys out of her pocket at the outside door to her building. Her heart was racing. She stood waiting for the elevator, glancing back at the front door every few seconds, as if she expected the big guy to come crashing through.

She stood in the left back corner of the elevator in combat stance, ready to fight anyone who appeared, but when the elevator opened on her floor, the hallway was quiet and empty. She was beginning to feel pain now, pain all over her body, but she didn't stop hurrying until she was double locked inside her apartment.

She crouched, her hands on her knees, while she got her breathing under control. She went into the bathroom, stripped off her clothes, and looked in the mirror. Bruise growing angry on her chin. Welts all over her chest and abdomen. One of those guys must have been wearing rings. She felt the knot on the back of her head and came away with a splotch of blood on the palm of her hand. She went into the kitchen and got down the bottle of vodka from the top shelf of the cabinet next to the refrigerator. What was she doing? Why hadn't she thrown that bottle away after she'd straightened herself out? But she was on autopilot, not thinking, her hands getting down a glass, twisting off the cap, pouring.

She went back into the bathroom. She filled the bath with cold water and got in, two fingers of vodka in the glass in her hand. She sipped the vodka, felt the heat run down her throat. She'd never seen the big guy before, she was sure of that. But the small guy? Was he one of the guys who'd attacked her the first time? Back when she'd come out of the neighborhood bar drunk and angry? There'd been two of them. Not expecting resistance. She would probably have killed them if they hadn't run. She looked at the vodka. Why was she drinking this? She set the glass on the floor outside the bath and slid down under the water.

When she rolled out of bed in the morning, she felt stiff and sore. She showered and took three ibuprofen and two Tylenol. The bruise on her chin didn't look quite as bad as she thought it might. She got dressed, put makeup on over the bruise, and tried to stand up straight when she walked. By the time she got into the office, Blunt was already at his computer. "Whoa, Doc, big night? Your coffee is probably cold."

He swiveled his chair toward her and frowned. "That makeup isn't getting the job done."

She sat down at her desk. "I'm okay."

"I thought you had a date with Frank last night."

"I did."

"What happened to your face?"

She filled him in.

"So when I saw you fighting the three guys, that was the second time you got jumped?"

She nodded.

"The first time was a few weeks before that on the way home from your neighborhood bar?"

"Yeah."

"That incident didn't cause you to reevaluate your behavior?"

"It's a free country. Assholes don't get to decide where I can go. I wasn't looking for trouble."

"Okay, okay. You're right. But the fallout is your neighborhood rapist holding a grudge. What are you going to do?"

"I'll figure it out. Don't worry. I'll be ready the next time."

They spent the day going through files, trying to find out as much as they could about Marie Adamescu and any groups she might be associated with. They managed to track her comings and goings from Europe to America over the last year. Six trips into Philadelphia, two trips into Chicago, one trip into Boise, Idaho. But her activities in Europe were a blank. Tina contacted the FBI to knock on doors and work contacts, but they were starting from scratch. Adamescu was still the mystery woman.

Midafternoon, Blunt called KD over to his desk. "Have a look at this."

She rolled her chair over to look at his computer screen. He pressed play. They were watching grainy surveillance camera footage on the street in her neighborhood. There she was, walking down the sidewalk, the man with the dog walking by, two guys on the other side of the street. They notice her, cross behind her, slip up on her.

"Where did you get this?"

"Our girl Tina. Some houses along there have private security cameras. She tapped into their feeds. No muss, no fuss."

"You told Tina?"

"What are friends for, Doc? We have to make sure these guys aren't connected to our investigation. She also hacked into hospital emergency room records. Guy who said he was in a bar fight had bruised balls and a bad bite to his nose. Required stitches. Has insurance from work. And he happens to live a few blocks from the scene of the crime."

"So you know his name, where he lives, and where he works. This is so illegal."

"Maybe I misunderstood. Did you just attack some random dudes because you were drunk and angry, or did you put a beating on this guy and his buddy because they tried to rape you?"

"I did not just jump some guys out of my neighborhood bar."

"So this guy is a rapist asshole."

"I can take care of this myself."

"Huh-uh. No lone-wolfing around here. We take care of our own. Can't have you walking around looking over your shoulder waiting for this guy and his next best friend."

"What have you got in mind?"

"Assess the threat. We have a look in his place, see if we can find out just how big a jerk this guy is."

After work, they sat in an old Camry on the street a few doors down from Jack Morrison's rowhouse. Blunt had done a complete work-up on him. He worked at a machine shop. Belonged to a mixed martial arts club. No rap sheet. Not even any speeding tickets.

"You bored?" Blunt asked.

"I'm getting there," KD replied.

"Want to eat our dinner?"

"It's a little early."

"I know it's early. I'm bored."

She shrugged. He passed her a deli sandwich wrapped in wax paper. She glanced inside. "This is yours. It's a Ruben."

They traded. KD ate her tuna salad sandwich and washed it down with a Diet Coke. No one came in or out of Morrison's house. At dusk, a truck pulled up in front and honked the horn. Morrison, his face taped, shambled down his walk and got into the front seat.

"Finally," Blunt said.

They strolled down the sidewalk and up to the front door of Morrison's rowhouse. KD pressed the doorbell. No one came. She pressed it again. No dog barking. "All clear."

Blunt picked the lock.

"You learn how to do that in the army?"

"I wish. Would have come in handy many times."

He opened the door. "After you."

They turned on the lights. The rowhouse was in good shape for a rental. The furnishings were simple. Sofa, two chairs, coffee table, and TV in the living room. Table with four chairs in the kitchen. Fenced backyard contained a covered barbeque grill and a motorcycle. Nothing out of place, which seemed odd for a single guy.

Upstairs, two bedrooms and a bathroom, one with a queen-size bed, the other with a desk and laptop computer. KD searched the bedroom. TV on the wall facing the bed. Bong leaning against a night table. Bloody clothes in a laundry basket in the closet. A lighter and a TV remote in the night table drawer. No women's clothes or underwear anywhere. She went into the bathroom. Men's shaving and shower supplies. One towel on the towel bar. The shower looked as if it had been cleaned recently.

KD found Blunt in the home office. Bondage porn photos were taped to the wall behind the desk. "That's got to mean something. Find anything?"

Blunt shook his head. "Usual paperwork. Receipts that need to be filed." He pointed to the laptop sitting on the desk. "Couldn't find the computer password written anywhere."

"Nothing to go with those photos?"

"Lots of folks pretend at that shit. Just like folks who dress up like animals."

"But we know this guy is violent."

"There's nothing here."

She looked in the closet. Martial arts gear, a blow-up mattress, sheets, and two pillows. Extra towels. Toilet paper on the top shelf. "There's got to be something."

"Guy's not a mastermind."

They turned off the lights and locked the door behind them. On the sidewalk walking toward them were two black police officers.

The officer on the right, a thin man with a mustache, spoke. "Sir, ma'am, do you live here?"

"No," Blunt replied. "Is there a problem?"

"Neighbor reported suspicious activity."

The other officer cut in. "How did you get in?"

"The door was open," Blunt said.

"The door was open?"

"That's right."

The first officer took over. "You're going to give us some answers or you're going to the station."

"I'm reaching for my ID," Blunt said. He reached into the inside pocket of his sports coat and handed the officer his NDA identification card.

"National Defense Agency?"

"We're on an active investigation."

"Of what?"

"Let me put it this way. When we find who we're looking for, it's more likely they're going to a black site than to the county jail."

"Is that so?"

"Lots of crazy white boys running loose."

The officer handed back the ID. "This is really about terrorists?"

Blunt nodded.

"Get out of here."

KD and Blunt strolled down the sidewalk to their Camry. The cops were still standing in front of Morrison's house. KD shook her head. "Crazy white boys? Think they'll check your story?"

"I don't care. Everything I said was the truth."

"Garcia might not see it that way."

"Let me worry about Garcia." Blunt checked his side mirror and pulled out into the street. "Drop you off at your place?"

"Yeah."

"You going to stay in, or do I need to be following you?"

"I'm not going out drinking."

"I believe you."

"Seriously. I haven't gone out drinking since I took this job."

"Glad to hear it." He stopped at the curb in front of her building. "See you tomorrow."

"What are we going to do about Morrison?"

"We'll figure it out."

After KD got into her apartment, she hung up her suit and put her shirt and underwear into the laundry basket in the floor of her closet. She carried her nightgown into the bathroom, hung it up on the robe hook, and looked at herself in the mirror. It was a good thing Frank wouldn't be back in town for three more weeks. Her body was still dotted with bruises. The swelling on her chin had gone down, but Blunt had been right. The makeup hadn't really been effective at hiding the bruise.

One step forward and two steps back. Isn't that what Frank had said? Was she going to hide the truth of things? She'd been hesitant about letting Frank into her apartment. Was she afraid that if he came up here, he'd see the last little bits of who she was, that she's be unable to hide her most inner self? Spin her life? Have one last place where she was accountable to no one? She rubbed lotion onto her arms and legs and pulled her nightgown on over her head. She needed to figure out what she was going to do.

MEANWHILE, Morrison was sitting at a corner table in the juice bar of the Ultimate MMA Training Club, talking with his buddies Bruce Drake, a small man with shaggy sandy-brown hair, and Paul Gibson, a huge muscled-up guy with a shaved head.

"How's your nose?" Drake said.

"Healing."

"And your balls?" Gibson chuckled.

"Ha, ha, ha. You remember how hard the bitch was, Bruce? Kicked the fuck out of us."

"You don't have to remind me. I'm still limping."

"Never thought I'd see her again. But there she was. Fat lot of good it did. Paul couldn't even slow her down."

"If she hadn't run, we would have fucked her bloody and left her in the weeds."

"We can still find her," Morrison said. "The three of us. As soon as I'm back in top shape."

"But we're not going to wait that long to catch some strange?" Gibson asked.

"No, couple of days. I won't be ready to work a bar until my nose is right, but I'll be ready for street work. I've got a couple of fresh spots scoped out."

"Can't wait," Drake said.

. . .

ON A TREE-LINED STREET IN BARCELONA, Marie Adamescu sat at an outdoor table at a crowded café. She wore an olive hunting jacket, jeans, walking shoes, and a brunette wig pulled back in a colorful scarf. A machine pistol sat in the small of her back under her jacket. She reached into a pocket, pulled out a pack of cigarettes and lit one. Across the table from her sat a clean-shaven Arab dressed like a tourist. "Cigarette?"

The man shook his head. "Do you have the nerve agent?" He spoke Catalan with a French accent.

Marie took a sip of coffee. "It's where I can get it, but this is a special weapon, not something that can be sold to just anyone. I need to hear more about your plans."

The Arab glanced at the nearby tables. "We need to talk somewhere more private."

She set some money on the table. "Follow me."

They meandered along the crowded sidewalk, crossed the street at the first intersection, and stopped on the street at the entry to an alley. "So," she said, "tell me more."

"I can't discuss the details. All I can say is that we have people in place close to a number of important targets. The French will learn the price of their hatred of the Prophet. They will feel the pain we feel."

A flash-bang went off in the street a few feet away. Police in tactical gear came rushing in through the smoke. Marie swung her machine pistol out of her jacket, fired a short burst toward the nearest police, turned, saw a gap between two cars, ran across the street and into a bakery. The Arab was right behind her. She ran past the people standing at the counter, pushed through the door into the kitchen, ran past the work counters and the ovens, and through the door into the back alley. There were no cops in sight. She pointed the machine pistol at the Arab. "You're on your own."

He nodded and took off to the right. A moped sat against the wall next to a door, but it was padlocked with a thick chain. She jogged off to the left. At the street, she glanced both ways. No cops. She took off the wig, dropped it onto the pavement, and shook out her short blonde hair. Then she took off her jacket and turned it inside out. Now it was bright blue. She put it back on, slid the machine pistol under the jacket, and started down the street. As she walked, she used her phone to call a rideshare service.

At the corner ahead of her, two cops wearing facemasks and carrying automatic rifles were looking through the pedestrians on the sidewalk. She walked right by them. Her ride pulled up just after she reached the next corner.

"Jenie? Going down to La Nova Marbella?"

"Yes." She spoke Spanish using her French accent.

At the beach, she sat on a bench overlooking the ocean. She'd only set the meeting place with the Arab a half hour beforehand, but the police strike team had been right there ready for them. They must have been following him. Or he was an undercover agent? But for whom? She wasn't going to give him the chance to contact her again. She sat for a few minutes, watching a woman and two small children play in the sand at the edge of the water. Then she made her way down to the private docks, taking her time, making sure that no one was following her.

She keyed in the password at the gate and walked down the slip to the yacht she'd arrived on two days earlier. A stocky man wearing a ball cap stood on the deck. "Marie? All is well?"

She made her way up the gangplank. "Take me into Toulon."

She went below deck. After she closed the door to her cabin, she made a phone call.

"Spanish police laid an ambush."

"But you delivered the nerve agent?"

"No. I've still got it. I'm getting out of here."

"We'll have to find another buyer."

"I've never had trouble in Spain before," Marie said.

"Interpol maybe?"

"That would mean our American friends have gotten into some trouble."

"We'll look into it."

. . .

THE NEXT AFTERNOON, KD and Blunt sat across from Jacobs in an interview room in the basement of the National Defense Agency. Jacobs wore an orange jump suit. McDonald's food wrappers sat on the table in front of him.

"You full now?" Blunt asked.

"Thanks," Jacobs said.

"You think your shoulders are broad enough to carry all the weight?"

"What are you talking about?"

"Automatic rifles, high explosives, detonator caps."

"I don't know how that stuff got there."

KD continued. "That's not what Bell said."

"He's a liar. He got involved with some bad people, got caught, and wants to blame it on the Patriot Alliance to get off."

"You don't want to take your chances with a jury."

"I'm innocent. There's no chance involved."

"Tomorrow you go back to Pennsylvania. You'll be on your own."

"Good."

KD and Blunt left the interview room. "He's the only one who hasn't taken a deal," KD said.

"He's the only one who actually knows anything," Blunt replied.

"Maybe a few more weeks in lockup will make it all seem real."

They took the elevator up to their office. A manila envelope with Tina's return address was sitting in Blunt's IN tray. Inside was a printed note and a magnetic keycard. "Morrison has a storage locker. We should take a look."

KD sat down at her desk. "What's our play here, Blunt?"

"What are we going to do when we finish investigating your boy?"

"Exactly. We're not going to kill him."

"Never said we would."

"We don't have any evidence that we can take to the police. It was all obtained illegally."

"Let's think this through," Blunt replied. "The first time this guy and some nameless buddy came after you, they came out of a bar following a lonely drunk girl and got surprised. The second time—do they know where you live or was it sheer coincidence? Your boy and a different running buddy walking along, maybe looking for an easy target, see you, want payback, come in hard. You messed them up again, got away. Does your boy want to avoid you, or does he have a hard on for you now? We don't know. But what we do know is this guy is poison. He's a serial rapist. He needs to be stopped."

"How?"

"I don't know yet. Maybe we'll figure it out when we know more."

"But we're not killing him."

"Only in self-defense."

That evening, they drove out to the Fortress Storage Warehouse, which was on a side street near a beltway interchange. A ten-foot chain-link fence topped with razor wire surrounded the property. Blunt pulled up to the gate and inserted the keycard into the card reader. The double chain-link gates rolled apart. Blunt glanced at KD after he pulled the keycard out. "If Tina gives you any tech, you know it's right."

"I can see three cameras from here. They're going to have this car and us on their hard drive."

"Standard tech. The picture will be grainy as hell, especially at night. And civilians don't have the kind of software that could clean it up."

They parked in front of the warehouse and put on throwaway gloves, used the keycard to open the outer door, and walked down the wide hallway, reading the numbers on the garage-size lockers. "Here it is," KD said.

A heavy-duty padlock locked the garage-style door. KD positioned herself between the padlock and the nearest surveillance camera. Blunt picked the lock and put the lock into his pocket before he lifted the door a quarter of an inch.

"Doc, see any wires attached to the bottom of the door?"

She got down in an elbow plank pose in front of the door and shined a penlight along the weather strip. "No."

"Out of the way, just in case."

She stood with her back against the wall. Blunt slowly raised the door. No boobytrap. The light from the hall shined in on a jumble of stored items. KD found the light switch. Blunt lowered the door behind them.

"Wonder what goes on here?" KD said.

"Nothing good," Blunt replied.

An old metal office desk sat in the middle of the space, an inkjet printer sitting on top. A row of printer paper boxes sat on a set of shelves to their right, along with camping gear and a well-worn backpack. A kid's bike with training wheels, two floor lamps, and a boxer's heavy bag were leaning against the back wall. More boxes were stacked on the left.

KD went to the shelves and started going through the papers in the boxes. Old receipts, product manuals, a lot of paperwork that should have been thrown away. Blunt looked through the desk drawers. Pencils and pens, a stapler, a roll of tape—the file drawer was empty. They started going through the boxes on the left. Old clothes, hiking boots, more violent porn photos.

KD found a pair of women's panties. "Blunt, come here." He looked over her shoulder. "That look like blood to you?"

Lacy pink panties with a row of dark flecks running across one side. "Let's lay out what's in this box," Blunt said.

They spread the contents of the box onto the floor. Men's clothes —long sleeve shirt, faded jeans, running shoes, the panties, and three porn photos. They squatted in front of them. "See any more blood?" KD asked.

Blunt pointed to the fly on the jeans. There was a dark stain along the edge of the zipper. KD smoothed out the shirt. Another stain on the shirt tail. Blunt picked up the photos and looked through them, studying each image.

"What?" KD asked.

"You remember the photos at Morrison's house?"

"Yeah."

"These are not like them."

"What do you mean?"

"Those were models, okay? They were posed, their eyes were

open, they were looking into the camera. And they were tied up. Look at these."

KD looked through the photos. All three were of the same woman. No ropes. Eyes closed. Mouth hanging open. In one of the photos she was wearing panties.

KD looked up at Blunt. He nodded. "This girl has been drugged."

"And the underwear in this picture looks like—"

"The ones right there."

"These are trophies," KD said.

"Looks that way."

"But he didn't drug me."

"You were drunk, weren't you? Maybe he thought that was enough advantage. Maybe he only drugs them if he knows them. Erase the memory."

They went through three more boxes, carefully unpacking and repacking the contents. His clothes, one item of women's underwear, three pictures in each one. "This is one fucked-up puppy," Blunt said. "You still against killing him?"

"I'm not a murderer, Blunt."

"There's murder, and then there's justice."

She shook her head.

"Suit yourself." He glanced at his watch. "We've been here a long time. We need to get going."

"Let's take these boxes."

"What if he come here and sees they're gone?"

"Better than him figuring out we're onto him and getting rid of them."

They carried the boxes out to the Camry. "I'll store the boxes in my tool shed," Blunt said. "I'm out of the loop."

"What about your wife or your kids? Won't they want to know what's in them?"

"My wife knows the drill, and my kids are in high school. They're not going anywhere near the tool shed."

9

Marie Adamescu sat in a booth in the back of a tourist bar in Munich, Germany, a glass of white wine in front of her and her eyes on the door. The place was modeled on an old-fashioned rathskeller, with heavy wooden furniture and beer-drinking murals on the plaster walls. There was soccer on the TV behind the bar, ten kinds of German beer on tap, and a lot of people speaking English and Chinese. When a nondescript man with gray hair and a tan raincoat came in, she gave him a nod.

He sat down opposite her, smiled, and reached across the table to squeeze her hand. "I heard Barcelona was a close thing."

"Ah, Tomas, always right to business."

"It's for the best."

"It was not too difficult. I maintained my cover with the Arab."

"And he escaped."

"Yes. We'll have to find out if he was a police agent. And we'll need some other way to turn public opinion against immigrants for the next French election."

Tomas nodded and then looked down at the table. "Something unfortunate we have to discuss."

"Go on."

"Your American has been arrested. His people have all turned."

"I know him. He won't talk."

"We know he's your pet, that you've been grooming him, but he's not important to our plans."

"In a few more years he could be. He could be the one to open our front in the US."

"I'm sorry. Decisions have been made."

"I'm sorry, too."

"Is this a problem for you?"

"No, no one person is more important than our work."

"I knew you'd see it that way."

"Have you found someone to buy the nerve agent?"

"We have a contact in Italy. His plans are probably more corporate than political, but he will serve his purpose." He took a folded-up paper from his coat pocket and handed it across the table.

Marie held it in her fist. "Anything else I need to know?"

"It's all there. Good luck, my darling."

Tomas got up and disappeared out onto the street. Marie sipped her wine. The soccer noise and the sea of foreign conversation were now somehow annoying. Marty was dead. Or he was going to be dead. What a waste. He was a true believer. A couple of years in a white power prison gang would have ground the soft edges off him, made him even more valuable. She got up, went into the ladies' room, opened the window, and climbed out into the alley. She hadn't been followed to the bar, but she didn't know if someone had managed to follow Tomas. Just to be safe, she was going to circle around a few blocks before she headed back to her hotel.

WEDNESDAY AFTERNOON, Martin Jacobs was back in the Buckwall County jail in Franklin Ford. He was sitting in the day room at a table with his back to the wall, reading a magazine. He expected his lawyer at two o'clock. He hadn't had any trouble since he'd been here. The blacks stayed away from him, and he stayed away from them. Word had gotten out that he was a stand-up guy, the kind of guy who wouldn't squeal, and that had carried him a long way. Everyone respected that.

Eric Bell strolled over, but he didn't sit down. "Hey, Marty."

"Fuck off."

"It's not personal, Marty. I always respected you. I still believe in the cause. I just didn't see any reason to go to jail for some foreigners. I'm getting out today."

"Good riddance."

"I know you're pissed at me. I just wanted to tell you that if you need anything, give me a call, and I'll hook you up."

"Get lost."

Bell shrugged. "All the same, I'll help if I can."

Jacobs watched him walk away. When Bell got about halfway across the dayroom, two black men scrambled up from their table, punched him to the floor, and started kicking him. The alarm sounded. The loudspeaker ordered everyone back to their cells. Jacobs got up, moving quickly out of the dayroom and down the hall, keeping an eye out for anyone coming too near.

As Jacobs passed an open cell three doors before his, a man sprang out into the hallway, grabbed his arm, and jabbed him four times in the belly with a sharpened toothbrush. Then he put his arm around Jacobs's shoulders, walked him down to his cell, and laid him on his cot. The man glanced into the hall. No one. He jammed the toothbrush through Jacobs's ear into his brain. Then he pulled it out and hustled back into his own cell. When the guards came down the hallway in riot gear, checking the cells, they found Jacobs dead.

ON THURSDAY MORNING, KD and Blunt got a call from Garcia. "Whoever got the nerve agent is tying up loose ends. McCuller, Dayton, and now Jacobs. And no leads on who got to Jacobs."

"And we're still nowhere on Marie Adamescu," KD said. "We're pretty sure she got out of the US, but we don't know how, and we don't know where she went. We don't even know her real name."

"FBI any help?" Garcia asked.

"The field reports are still coming in," Blunt said. "We know she's been meeting with Fatherland Volk white nationalists. Two guys in Chicago and one guy in Boise."

"The Fatherland Volk. It makes a lot more sense that they'd be receiving weapons than a wannabe group like the Patriot Alliance," Garcia replied.

"So what does that make Jacobs and the Patriot Alliance?" KD asked. "A recruitment front?"

"Leftwing terrorists used to do the exact same thing back in the 1960s," Garcia said. "Funnel college kids into antiwar or civil rights groups that recruited for terrorist cells."

"Well, Jacobs won't be telling us anything now," KD said.

"Maybe one of the others we arrested knows something," Blunt replied.

"Maybe," Garcia said. "I'll have Tina check the database for connections between the Fatherland Volk and European rightwing groups. Maybe we'll have some luck there. You two keep following the trail you're on. Anything else?"

"No, boss."

Garcia ended the call.

Blunt shook his head. "Keep after it from our end? We don't have any leads."

"Let's have another look at the interview transcripts of everyone arrested with Jacobs. Maybe we missed something."

A few hours later, Blunt rubbed his eyes and pushed back from his computer screen. "Finding anything?"

KD turned toward him. "No, nothing helpful."

"Change of subject," Blunt said. "You given any more thought to our boy Morrison?"

"Yeah. We should have a look at the mixed martial arts studio."

"Why?"

"Because he wasn't by himself."

"Have you looked at the website?"

She shook her head.

"No women in the pictures. Just a lot of macho testosterone bull-shit. Somebody's probably dealing growth hormone out of there."

At four o'clock, they were parked on the street with a good view of the entrance to Ultimate MMA Training Club. Men dressed from work—some casual office, some work clothes—trickled in. An hour later, a few men started to trickle out. Around six-thirty, a big guy with a shaved head, muscles bulging through his clothes, came around the corner and pushed through the door.

"That was the guy with Morrison the other night."

"You sure?"

"Absolutely."

"He's the guy who blindsided you?"

"Yep."

"You really were lucky to get away."

"I don't mind admitting I was scared. I was running full out."

Thirty minutes later, a truck pulled into an open parking spot in front of the club and Morrison, his face taped, got out of the passenger's side. The driver had shaggy, sandy-brown hair and walked with a limp. Blunt chuckled. "That some of your work?"

"It's been awhile, but that's probably the guy from my first run-in with Morrison."

At ten o'clock, several men left, and the outside lights were turned off, but Morrison and his two buddies were still inside.

"Who owns this gym?" KD asked.

"Not one of them."

"They must have a key."

At 10:45 p.m., Morrison and his friends came out of the club. The big guy jogged off around the corner and came back driving a Honda CR-V. Morrison and the other guy got in.

"You think they're going to show us who they are?" KD asked.

"Let's find out."

Blunt fell in half a block behind them. KD felt for her Glock. If they'd been spotted, if they were driving into a trap, she wasn't going hand-to-hand again. The Honda drove past a bus that was stopped at a bus stop. Several black women dressed in fast-food uniforms got off and walked away into a neighborhood of small houses, chatting as they moved along. The Honda circled the block. Only two of the women were still on the main thoroughfare. The Honda circled around again. The women were gone. The Honda cut down a side street. One woman, by herself, was walking down the sidewalk. Her lips were moving like she was talking on her phone.

The Honda pulled over. Shaggy got out, pulled a dark-colored ballcap down on his head, and started up the street after the woman. The Honda drove off. Blunt pulled over on the other side of the street. "You carrying?"

"Yeah. You?"

"Always."

KD reached for the door handle. "You ready?"

"Hang on, Doc. Recon only. We don't want to tip our hand unless we have to."

"They're going to grab her."

"She might turn into any one of these yards."

"Okay."

Blunt turned off the inside light. They slipped out of the car and positioned themselves where they could watch what was happening on the other side of the street. Shaggy was gaining on the woman. And now the big guy was walking toward her, black ball cap, head down, hands in his pockets, moving toward the outer edge of the sidewalk, as if he wanted to give her room. KD was in a crouch, ready to spring up running.

"Hey, white boy." An old black man, gray beard and bald head, stood up from a dark porch. "You lost?" He stepped down onto the top step, the streetlight shining off his head. He had a phone in his hand. "Why you following that girl? You don't belong in this neighborhood. I'm calling the police."

Shaggy turned and ran. The big guy crossed the street. KD and Blunt got back in their car. The big guy walked up the sidewalk and crossed over to the Honda, which drove off around the corner. Blunt pulled away from the curb. "What do you think, Doc, amateurs or hard guys? They going to keep hunting or are they done for the night?"

He followed the Honda around the block. They watched Shaggy get into the back seat. The Honda drove three blocks and pulled into a Convenience Mart. Shaggy went in and came out with a six-pack in a bag. Then the Honda drove back to the Ultimate MMA Training Club. Shaggy and Morrison got back in the truck. The truck and the Honda drove off in different directions.

"What do you want to do about these fellas, Doc?"

"I don't know."

"These boys are assholes of the worst kind. Your boy Morrison, we know he's got to go down, but I'm thinking these other two got to go as well."

"You're right, getting rid of Morrison wouldn't stop those guys, not permanently. Could Tina find out who the other guys are and where they live?"

"She could probably pull some security footage somewhere."

"Let's see what she can find out." She sighed. "Nothing else we can do today. I'm bushed. Can you drop me at home?"

"You bet."

KD went into the lobby of her building and waited until Blunt had driven away. Then she walked down the street to her neighborhood bar, the place where she had first encountered Morrison and his friend. She didn't know why she was going there. She knew she shouldn't have a drink, not in that bar, not where the trouble began, but her feet carried down the sidewalk just the same.

The bar was the typical sort of neighborhood place, long bar with foot rail down one side, some tables in the open area, and a pool table at the back. She counted nine people spread out in the space. Four at the bar, three at one table, a man and woman playing pool. A man she vaguely recognized nodded at her. She nodded back.

She stepped up to the bar. The bartender, a dark-haired woman with tattoos of palm trees on her forearms, smiled. "What can I get you?"

"Rum and Coke."

The bartender set the drink in front of her. She handed her a twenty-dollar bill, then took the thin straw out of the drink and had her first sip. The bartender set her change on the bar in front of her.

Morrison and his buddies. She felt the blackness creep over her. Finding the trophies was one thing, but seeing those guys hunt that woman, she felt—she didn't know what she felt. She just wanted to stop feeling it. She drained her drink and motioned to the bartender.

"Another?"

She nodded.

The bartender fixed the rum and Coke, brought it to her, and took payment from the cash on the bar. KD nodded and took a drink. The cold liquid felt good going down, but it didn't make her feel any better. She looked in the mirror behind the bar. No one was watching her. Why was she in here? Nothing good was going to come of this, although she didn't feel angry. She just felt that emptiness and worth-lessness she'd first felt when Frank left. She hadn't really believed he'd do it. He'd made his ultimatum. And then he did exactly what he said he'd do. Him being back didn't make up for that feeling of betrayal.

She took another drink. But why was she feeling that now? Why did Morrison and his buddies trigger those feelings? Why did she feel like she'd betrayed herself? Was it about those guys, or was it about having Frank back in her life? Was she taking the easy way out taking him back? Giving up on finding a new man who hadn't hurt her, might not hurt her, at least wouldn't hurt her as much as he had.

Or was that all just bullshit? He was right. There was magnetism between them. The magnetism of shared history, of shared knowing, of shared triumphs and disappointments. It was easy to fall under that old spell. But did that make it wrong? She sighed. Drinking wasn't going to help. She had a full day tomorrow. The chance to make a difference, or at least to try to find a way to take those rapists off the street. She left a couple of dollars on the bar and walked out into the night.

.   .   .

BLUNT SAT in his car down the street from the bar, watching for KD. The evening was quiet. Most people were already at home for the night. When she came out, he started the engine, let her get across the intersection, and followed slowly behind her, arriving at her apartment building just as she went back inside. She shouldn't have gone into that bar. Morrison and his crew could have shown up. Still, she didn't look hypervigilant. She probably hadn't been looking for trouble. And this evening had been pretty intense. Hell, he was going to have a few drinks when he got home, and he had his wife to talk with. She probably just wasn't ready to be alone. Still, he'd promised Garcia he'd have KD's back until they got this business squared away.

He pulled over and waited. The lights came on in her apartment. No reason to be here anymore. Time to go home.

THE NEXT MORNING, they received a report from the FBI along with security camera footage that showed Marie Adamescu getting on a private plane at a private airfield in New Jersey eight days ago. The flight plan indicated that the plane landed at an airstrip outside Madrid, but there were no cameras at that location.

"She was way ahead of us," KD said.

"If she had the nerve agent, she got it out of the country before we even knew about Jacobs," Blunt replied.

"Just makes it all the more likely Jacobs landed on the loose ends list as soon as he was picked up."

"There's got to be a thread we can follow."

"Maybe the FBI has something new on Adamescu's Chicago and Idaho contacts. Let's check the report log."

AT 11:00 a.m. Garcia was sitting in her office on an encrypted video call with the National Defense Agency Berlin station chief, a stocky man who looked like a banker. "What have you got for me?"

"Your target—Marie Adamescu, or whatever her name is—is definitely associated with the People's Freedom Party."

"I've got some vague idea of who they are. Refresh my recollection."

"Underground militant group that works across Europe. They've infiltrated several rightwing political parties. They're connected to crimes against immigrants—fires, bombings, assaults, riots at counter demonstrations."

"Do you know where she is?"

"We're working on it. We caught her on a surveillance camera in Munich three days ago, but then we lost her. Most cities in Europe are covered by cameras, but it's still hard to find a particular person in real time."

"How long?"

"We're branching out from that sighting. Could take several days, or we could get lucky and get a hit in the next few minutes that narrows down the search."

"Keep me informed. And send me everything you've got on the People's Freedom Party." Garcia ended the call and then called KD.

"Hey, boss," KD said, "I've got you on speaker with Blunt."

"I heard back from our Berlin office. Adamescu was sighted in Munich three days ago."

"So she's been moving across Europe."

"I'll be forwarding you a file on the People's Freedom Party in the next few minutes. Be ready to travel. And in the meantime, keep digging into Adamescu's connections with the Fatherland Volk."

AFTER LUNCH, KD and Blunt got an email from Tina. She'd tracked down Morrison's running buddies. Attached were their pictures and information. Shaggy was Bruce Drake. He was a plumber's apprentice. No record. The big guy, Paul Gibson, worked for a moving company. He was on probation for selling anabolic steroids. KD pulled up their addresses on google maps.

"How do you want to use this info?" Blunt asked.

"We've got Morrison's trophies. How about if we spread them out in these guys's houses and get the cops to search the houses?"

"How?"

"I'm just thinking out loud, okay?"

"Wouldn't be too hard to get Gibson picked up. He's on probation. But the charge would need to stick to keep him off the streets."

"For Morrison, we could call 911, report a break-in. If the door was open when the police got there, they'd go in."

"But they wouldn't look in boxes."

"So we'd have to lay the trophies out on the table, like he was going through them."

"Let me get this straight. We're going to set the evidence out and call the cops."

"What else can we do? They're hunting women. We've got to get them off the streets before they hurt anyone else."

"What about the other guys?"

"We leave their names and pictures there. Put a trophy box in each of their houses."

"I can think of a dozen ways this plan could foul up."

"If this plan doesn't work, we'll have to step up to something more aggressive."

That evening, KD and Blunt were parked on the street where they had a good view of the front doors of the Ultimate MMA Training Club. Just like clockwork, Drake and Morrison drove up in Drake's truck just after Gibson came around the corner and went in.

"Let's get it done," KD said.

They drove over to Morrison's rowhouse. No one was on the street. The lights were on next door, but they couldn't see any shadows moving in the living room. They put on throw-away gloves before they got out of the car. Blunt popped the trunk. They each picked up one of the printer paper boxes and carried them to Morrison's front door, where Blunt set his box down to pick the door lock.

Once inside, they turned on the lights. Blunt did a quick walk-through. KD went to the kitchen table. She'd brought the box they'd opened first in the storage locker. She laid out the pictures, placing the panties next to the picture of the woman wearing them, and arranged the men's clothes so that the dry blood was as obvious as possible. Then she set the other box on the end of the table, took the top off, and made sure the pictures were on top facing up. She left Drake's and Gibson's photos lying on the floor as if they'd fallen off the table.

Blunt came down the stairs. "Everything's the same as last time." He looked at what she'd done. "Ready to go?"

She nodded. They left the front door slightly ajar, hurried back out to their car and drove away. KD took out a burner phone and input 911. "I'm walking my dog. There's a door open on a house I always walk by. I went up and rang the bell, but no one answered." She gave Morrison's address and ended the call.

"Pull the chip," Blunt said.

"The call wasn't long enough to trace."

"Don't care."

KD pulled the chip from the phone and tossed it out the window. Then she got out her smartphone and input Gibson's address, which turned out to be a tiny house on a street near an apartment complex. An old Dodge minivan was parked in the driveway. They could see a woman through the kitchen window, making motions as if she was washing dishes. They slipped out of the Camry and sneaked up to the side of the house. The woman, narrow face, limp light brown hair, was smoking a cigarette while she worked. A fresh bruise marked her cheek. KD and Blunt crept back out to the Camry. "This is no good," Blunt said.

"We should have done more research," KD replied. "Let me check out Drake's house."

She pulled up the county assessor's database on her phone and put in Drake's address. It was a middleclass home in a neighborhood of property owners. Shelly and Nicholas Drake were the longtime owners. "He lives with his parents."

Blunt shook his head. "Why am I not surprised?"

"Time's wasting. We need to get back to the training gym before they leave there."

When they parked across from the Ultimate MMA Training Club,

Drake's truck was still parked out front. "What was Gibson driving last night?" Blunt asked.

"Dark blue Honda CR-V."

"Was it his car or did he pick it up somewhere?"

"What're you getting at?"

"We couldn't get into their houses, but we could put the trophies into their vehicles. We just don't want to put a box of trophies into the back of a car he's going to ditch."

"How are you going to break into their cars? There aren't any door locks to pick."

"You need to get up to speed, Doc. I don't have to pick the car door locks. I've got an app on my phone that mimics car key fobs. Agency issue. I chose the brand, the app acts like the fob."

"How long have they had that?"

"Don't know. Used to have to use a small tablet computer. This is a lot more convenient."

"Okay. Let's give it a try. Gibson came around from the side of the building both times. I'll text you if they come out the front."

Blunt popped the trunk before he got out of the car. He picked up one of the printer paper boxes, walked down to the corner, and crossed with the walk sign. A row of cars was parked in metered parking along the side of the building. No Honda CR-V. No dark blue SUV. He scanned the other side of the street. No parking. He thought about Gibson jogging around the corner, really into his pace, not like he was just coming a few steps. Blunt continued past the driveway at the back of the club. Cars were parked at the curb in front of the houses, but there were no parking meters. The street sign indicated there was on-street parking from 6:00 p.m. to 8:00 a.m. And there it was, Gibson's Honda. Parked two driveways down.

Blunt glanced around. There was no one on the street. Lights were on in the house directly in front of the Honda, but no one was visible. He set the box on the street behind the Honda, took out his phone, opened the fob app, chose Honda. A dot on the app filled in, and the liftback popped open. Blunt put his phone away and took another look around. Then he pushed the box into the righthand corner nearest the taillight, pushed an old blanket up against it, and closed the liftback. As he was stepping back up onto the sidewalk, he heard a voice.

"Hey, man, hold up."

A twenty-something wearing a hoodie and jeans was walking down the steps from the house. Blunt waited but he didn't say anything.

"This your car?"

"Uh-huh," Blunt replied.

"You're always parking in front of my house, which means my wife has to circle the block looking for a place when she gets home from work. Can you park somewhere else?"

"The signs don't say resident only."

"I know, but that's how it works around here."

"Okay. This is the last time. I promise."

The man nodded. "Okay."

"A buddy of mine will be coming to collect the car later. After that, you won't see it again."

The man nodded and went back up to his house. Blunt continued to the end of the block and crossed the street to the Camry. He opened the car door, but he didn't get in. "One down."

He popped the trunk again, picked up the last box of trophies, waited for a break in the traffic, and hustled across the street to Drake's pickup truck. He stood on the street side of the truck and used his phone app again. A man and a woman, a dog pulling the leash in the man's hand, came around the corner, walking toward the truck. Blunt ducked. He heard their voices as they passed by, but he couldn't make out what they were saying. He glanced at the phone app. The dot had filled in. He opened the truck door and jammed the box in behind the driver's seat. The headlights on the Camry flashed. He pushed the truck door shut, crept along the side of the bed, and peeked around the end. Two guys were coming out of the club, but they weren't their guys. Blunt strolled up onto the sidewalk, crossed at the crosswalk, and walked back down to the Camry.

"Almost lost it when you flashed the lights," he said.

"If I'd have waited until I could see who it was, it would have been too late."

"Well, it's all done now."

They sat back in their seats, watching the entrance to the club, and waited.

THE TWO BLACK cops got out of their cruiser in front of Morrison's rowhouse. The house was dark inside, but they could see from the sidewalk that the door was ajar. The younger cop turned on his heavy flashlight. "Isn't this the house where we let that couple go the other day?"

The older cop turned his on as well. "Yep. Hope that wasn't a mistake."

They moved up the sidewalk, the younger cop in front, his free hand on his holstered gun, the flashlight shining in front of him. They couldn't hear any noise from inside the house.

"Give the door a little shove," the older cop said.

The younger cop pushed the door open. The only sound was the creaking of the hinges. They shined their flashlights into the living room. It appeared to be empty. "Police," he yelled.

No one answered. The younger cop banged on the door frame and yelled "Police" again before he stepped in, found the light switch, and turned on the lights. The living room was clear. "Upstairs?" the younger cop asked.

"Down here first."

They walked back into the kitchen. Two printer paper boxes sat on the table, both with their tops off. Photos and clothes were laid out in front of a chair as if someone had been sitting there examining them. The older cop stepped around the table, looked at the pictures, at the panties, and then at the pictures again. He looked up at his partner. "Don't touch anything."

"What is it?"

"Might just be some crazy fantasy thing, or it might be a crime scene. I'm calling it in."

. . .

MORRISON, Drake, and Gibson came out of the training club. Gibson disappeared around the corner and came back driving the Honda. Morrison got in the front, and Drake got in the back.

"You sure he won't be parking around the corner anymore?" KD asked.

"I'm hoping he'll be back in jail by morning."

The Honda drove east to the boulevard and then south for twenty minutes until it entered another neighborhood of modest, one-story houses. It parked across from a bus stop with a large shelter. KD and Blunt pulled to the curb half a block back.

"Same MO," Blunt said.

"They haven't got a care. Never check to see if they're being followed."

A bus pulled up. Several young white people got out. "What's the deal?" KD asked. "Mall employees and fast-food shift change?"

"Morrison and his buddies sure know which bus stops to watch."

Two young women, walking together, crossed the street and turned onto a side street. The Honda followed. Blunt trailed behind. The Honda stopped in the street. Blunt pulled over. Drake got out. He followed behind the women, giving them most of a block.

"What's going on?" KD asked. "They can't be planning to grab both of those girls."

"Morrison and his crew don't stand out in this neighborhood. So maybe they're setting up for an either-or situation."

Blunt pulled out. "Can you see the Honda?"

"It's got to be up ahead."

"Oh, shit, it's right in front of that painter's van."

KD ducked down in her seat as they drove by. After she scooted up, she saw Gibson step out onto the sidewalk. "There he goes. Just like last time."

Blunt sped around the block, and then slowed down to a crawl. The two young women were standing on the sidewalk. They hugged. One went into a house. The other continued down the block. Drake sped up, moving quietly, closing the gap from behind. Gibson strolled along, looking down, as if he was lost in thought.

"They're going to take this one," KD said.

"Look at her," Blunt replied. "Head up, chest out, firm step—she's not moving like prey."

"I see what you're saying—it's like she's trained up in some way. But there's still two of them. And Gibson's a giant."

The woman glanced over her shoulder, saw Drake close behind, put her hand into her jacket pocket and backed against a front yard fence. Blunt turned off the Camry's headlights and stopped at the curb half a block back. Gibson and Drake both turned to the woman as the Honda sped backward to their location. KD jumped out of the Camry. Gunshots. One, two, three. KD ducked back against the side of the car. Gibson dragged Drake toward the Honda. The woman ran out into the street after them, raised her arm and fired twice more before the Honda turned the corner.

KD ran toward the woman, yelling as she came. "Hey! Hey! You all right?"

The woman pointed the gun at her and then lowered it.

"That was some crazy shit," KD said.

The woman nodded. She was breathing hard.

KD looked up and down the street. "Put your gun back in your pocket."

The woman glanced down at the blackened bullet hole in her jacket pocket. Her voice was robotic. "Ruined my jacket." She slipped her gun back in her pocket, but she didn't let go of it.

"Were you expecting trouble?"

"Some guy came after me last year. After that I made myself a promise."

"Are you okay? You want a ride? My buddy and I just turned up this street. Saw the whole thing."

"You don't live around here."

"No, I don't. Just driving through."

"I'll be okay."

"You sure?"

"I said I'll be okay."

She was still standing on the sidewalk with her hand in her pocket when KD got back in the Camry and she and Blunt drove away.

"She had that blank look on her face like the PTSD was welling up," KD said.

"Well, she fucked them up. Hope she can deal with it." He screeched around the corner. "Let's see if we can catch up to them."

"Why? We know where they're going."

"Is one of them shot? Do they have a back-up plan?"

10

The Honda slid around the corner. Drake was shrieking from the back seat. "Fuck me, fuck me, fuck me," Morrison muttered. He glanced at Gibson. "How bad is he?"

Gibson had his right hand clamped over his left arm. Blood was tricking between his fingers. "I think he took two." He dug a rag out of the glove box, wrapped it around his arm, and used his teeth and his right hand to tie the knot. "Find someplace to pull over. Someplace without witnesses."

"I'm not an idiot."

Morrison saw a church up ahead, turned into the parking lot, and parked by a bank of bushes next to the dumpster. He turned to Gibson. "You watch."

Gibson got out and stood in the open door. Morrison climbed into the back seat with Drake. Drake was hyperventilating. His eyes had the look of an animal caught in a trap. Blood was leaking through his hands as he pressed down on his stomach. His shirt and the car seat were sopped with blood.

"Hold on there, buddy," Morrison said. "We'll get you fixed up."

"How is he?" Gibson asked.

"Shot in the belly, looks like. You got a first aid kit?"

"No."

"Where can we get one?"

Gibson shook his head. "This ain't no movie, bro. First aid kit isn't going to cut it."

Morrison looked up into Gibson's face.

"I won't tell," Drake said. "I'll keep my mouth shut. We didn't do anything."

"Hold on," Morrison said.

Morrison and Gibson got back in the front, Morrison still driving. They drove out of the church parking lot. "We can't kill him," Morrison said.

"Listen to yourself. Right now he's done for, but we're both still free."

"But he's right, we didn't do anything. There's no evidence. They find that girl, it's just her word. There's not a scratch on her, is there?"

"It's your call."

"Find the nearest hospital."

Gibson found a hospital on his smartphone. They pulled up to the emergency department. Gibson dragged Drake out onto the pavement. As they drove away, he called the hospital and told them Drake was on the driveway.

"What a clusterfuck," Morrison said.

"Get your shit together," Gibson said.

"Do we move Drake's truck or leave it in front of the club?"

"Leave it. We don't know anything about where he went or what he did. We left the club and went home. Find out what was on TV and read a synopsis just in case this blows back."

"Your wife going to cover for you?"

"If she knows what's good for her."

"What are you going to do about this car?"

"Wipe it down. Bleach the seat. I can't afford to get rid of it."

"Okay, I'll get out at The Shamrock Bar. I'm in there all the time. Someone will misremember when I got there. I'll have a beer and then catch a rideshare."

. . .

KD AND BLUNT turned in the same direction as they'd seen the Honda go and drove along looking down the side streets, but they were too late.

"Think they'll go back for Drake's truck tonight?" KD asked.

"Did Annie Oakley actually shoot anyone, or did she just scare the hell out of them?" Blunt replied.

"They were as close as me and you. Pretty hard to miss."

"Let's go sit on the truck for a little while. If Drake's going home tonight, he's taking that truck. If he doesn't take it, we can have Tina check the hospitals and the morgue for gunshot victims in the morning."

MORRISON GOT out of a rideshare a block away from his rowhouse. Even from here, he could see that two police cruisers were parked on the street in front of his place. How did they get here so fast? How had they connected him with Drake? It didn't matter. There was no evidence. They hadn't taken the girl. They'd taken Drake to the hospital. He just needed to keep his story straight. He went to the training club to hang out. Then he went to The Shamrock for a few beers. He took a rideshare home. He was walking to clear his head. What if they say your buddy says you brought him to the hospital? I didn't want to get involved. I didn't see anything—which was true.

He walked up the sidewalk to his rowhouse. All the lights were on and the front door was open. When he went into his living room, he could see crime scene technicians in their white coveralls in his kitchen.

"Mr. Morrison?"

Two black cops were standing in front of him. "Yeah, that's me. What's going on here?"

"Detective." The older cop hollered back into the kitchen. A woman wearing a navy pantsuit, a badge hanging from a chain around her neck, came into the room.

"Mr. Morrison?"

"Yes. What's going on here?"

"We got a 911 that your door was open. Officers did a walk-through on a probable break-in. They found evidence possibly connected to sexual assaults."

"What are you talking about?"

"Boxes containing pictures and blood-spattered clothes."

"That's insane." Morrison started walking toward the kitchen. The older black cop stepped in front of him.

"You can't go in there," the detective said. "You're going to have to come down to the station while we sort this out."

"I don't know what you're talking about."

"As soon as we have the fingerprint and DNA results, we'll know what's what. If you're innocent, you have nothing to worry about."

KD AND BLUNT sat in their car across the street from the Ultimate MMA Training Club, watching Drake's pickup truck until the last few people trickled out of the club and the lights went out.

"Looks like our boys chewed off more than they could swallow," Blunt said.

"Wonder what's going to happen next," KD replied.

"Guess we'll find out in the morning. We did our best to trip them up."

"Couldn't have done it without that woman."

Blunt chuckled. "Wild card. That's when you find out what you're made of."

"Glad they didn't measure up."

Blunt glanced in the rearview mirror and pulled away from the curb. "Want to get a drink? Unwind a little bit?"

"No, I'm good. You can drop me home."

"You sure you're good to go? That was some heavy shit tonight."

"I'm fine, Blunt. I'll admit I was having some trouble last night—those bastards tracking that woman—watching them, knowing they'd try again, my blood was up."

"I know what you mean. I was tossing and turning, thinking about what I'd do if someone attacked my daughter."

"But tonight? I'm feeling a little closure, like maybe we made some difference."

"I hear you."

"I'm fine, really."

"Okay, I'll drop you home."

MARIE ADAMESCU CAME out of a private bank in Bern, Switzerland, a duffel over her shoulder, and got into a cab. Across the street, a woman who was standing at a nearby bus stop spoke into her phone. "She just left the bank and got into a cab. I'm texting you the picture."

"No need. We've got her on the cameras."

"Where do you want me to go?"

"You're done. Go back to the office."

The National Defense Agency's Berlin station chief ended the encrypted call and made another one. "Stacy? Are you on her?"

"We've got her."

"TAKE ME TO THE TRAIN STATION," Marie Adamescu said as she climbed into the cab. She spoke in French-accented German. The cab driver nodded. She had noticed the woman at the bus stop when she came out of the bank. Maybe she was just being paranoid—there was nothing unusual about the woman—but she wasn't going to take any chances, not when she was this close to getting rid of the nerve agent. She'd had to hold on to it a lot longer than she had planned. And now she had to take it into Italy. Still, she had her new passport and credit cards. She hadn't been in contact with anyone. She'd been completely on her own since Munich, which made her almost untraceable.

The cab pulled up in front of the train station. People were streaming out of the glass-fronted building, and crowds were flowing across the lobby and up and down the escalators. Adamescu made her way to the rental lockers, got her roller case, and went into the nearest ladies' room, where she locked herself in a stall. She opened her roller case, switched to a casual jacket, and put on a long black wig. Then she went to the sink, styled the wig in the mirror, and accented it with a colorful scarf. She was lucky that her skin tone went with so many hair colors. She shouldered the duffel and pulled her roller bag out onto the concourse and headed for the platform for the train to Milan.

A FEW MINUTES LATER, Stacy and her four-person team were fanning out in the railway station, searching through the crowd, hunting for Adamescu. They knew she'd come in here. Stacy went into the first ladies' room and pushed open all the doors to the stalls. No one and no clues. Damn it. She went to the departures board. Four trains were departing in the next half hour. She pulled her people together. "One of you is going to be on each of those trains."

They all scurried off to buy tickets and rush for the platforms. She called Berlin Station. "We lost her."

"You better find her."

"I'm on it."

BACK AT THE National Defense Agency offices, right before lunch, KD and Blunt heard back from Tina. "Drake was left at the ER with gunshot wounds. Once he had adequate pain relief, he told the police he'd been out with Morrison and Gibson, but he couldn't remember how he got shot. The police caught up with Gibson this morning. His wife said he was home last night, but he had a probable gunshot wound to his arm, and there was blood in the back seat of his car. Guess he was planning to clean up when the light was good. That's when they found the box of rape trophies. They took him into custody. They also found Drake's truck, got a search warrant, and found that trophy box. So now he's handcuffed to his bed. Took the police until an hour ago to figure out Morrison was already in custody for the rape trophies found at his place. Cops are trying to connect them to old cases."

"Thanks, Tina."

"You bet."

KD ended the call.

"That was some good work there," Blunt said.

"Yes, it was. I'm glad we could take these assholes off the street. Feel more relieved than I thought I would. Thanks for butting in."

"We're partners, Doc. I've got your back. But no more getting drunk by yourself in dive joints. When you put you at risk, you put us at risk."

"I'm all straightened up, Blunt. Believe me."

"Want to go to lunch?"

"I need to finish reading this last report first."

"Adamescu's Idaho connection?"

"Yeah. I'm still hoping to find something of interest here."

She picked up her pencil, found the spot where she had left off, and then turned and looked at Blunt. "When you put you at risk, you put us at risk."

"That's what I said."

"Garcia sanctioned this little side project right from the beginning, didn't she?"

Blunt chuckled. "You're a quick study, Doc. That's what I told the boss."

"You're one sneaky bastard, Blunt."

"Thank you."

"Give me twenty minutes to finish this up."

"Take your time, Doc."

A FEW DAYS LATER, Marie Adamescu stood in a small park across from a church in Milan, Italy. Night was coming on, a slow drizzle was falling, and she was beginning to think her contacts weren't going to make it. Then two men appeared out of the fog across the street, an older man wearing a hat and an overcoat and a younger man wearing a leather jacket and heavy boots. They looked more like mafiosi than operatives, but they were the ones who'd won the bidding war for the nerve agent.

As they approached, the older man spoke in Italian-accented German. "Miss, I'm glad you waited. Traffic." He shrugged.

The younger man stood behind him and to his right, his hand obviously on a gun in his jacket pocket.

Adamescu replied in Italian. "Sometimes we make allowances in our work."

"Have you got the package?"

"It's close at hand. Here are the routing and account numbers." She handed him a piece of paper.

The older man took a smartphone out of his pocket and spent a few minutes inputting information. "All done."

Adamescu took out her phone and verified the money transfer. "Very good. Follow me."

She led them down the alley beside the church to a battered Fiat parked near the backdoor to a restaurant. She opened the trunk and unzipped a blue duffel. The man put his hand on the canister as if touching it could tell him what it was. Then he turned to his companion and nodded. The younger man zipped the duffel and shouldered it.

The older man looked at Adamescu carefully. "If all is as your people say, you will never see us again."

She smiled. "Good luck in your endeavors."

The two men walked back toward the park. Once they were out of sight, Adamescu went into the back of the restaurant, walked through a storeroom into the kitchen, squeezed by the servers waiting for their orders to come up, came out into the dining room, and made her way through the tables and out the front door onto the street. She stood for a moment, studying her surroundings. A couple walking hand-in-hand on the other side of the street. Two cars looking for parking spaces. Nothing to concern her.

She turned left, walked to the corner, and turned left again. Then she crossed at the corner, walked a block, and turned right. No one was following her. Still, just to be sure, she walked two more blocks before she stopped in front of another restaurant and ordered a cab to the Lancaster Hotel.

She unlocked the door to her hotel room. She'd gotten rid of the nerve agent. With Marty gone, there was no one to tie her to it. She had one more contact to meet with, tomorrow, early, and then she would be off to Germany. She took a pistol from her shoulder bag before she opened the door and turned on the lights. Everything was just as she left it, but she checked the bathroom and closet anyway. All clear.

The two she'd sold the nerve agent to did not inspire confidence. There was something about them, something that suggested carelessness. Never mind. They didn't know who she was or where she was, and she would not be findable tomorrow. She sat on the edge of the bed, set her pistol down, and pulled off her red wig. She was supposed to stay here overnight, but she had a nagging feeling that she wasn't safe in this hotel any longer. She got up and looked out the window. Cars drove by, people walked on the sidewalk—of course, if she was being watched, it would be from an apartment across the street. She got her roller bag out of the closet—she'd never unpacked—laid it on the bed and opened it. She went into the bathroom and fixed her hair and checked her makeup before she closed her shower kit, placed it in its spot in the roller bag, put the wet wig in a plastic bag, smoothed the bag across the clothes, and closed the roller bag. Time to go.

She took the elevator down, rolled her bag across the lobby and out onto the sidewalk. The sky was a swirl of dark clouds. No one was following her. Ahead, a line of people stood outside a bar where rock and roll pulsed out into the night. As she approached, a Range Rover pulled up to the curb. A woman stepped out of the passenger's side and waved toward two men and a woman standing in line to get into the bar. The closest man grabbed Marie's right arm, and the other man and the two women swarmed her and shoved her and her roller bag into the Range Rover, which sped away.

The two men, one of the women, and Adamescu were crushed together in the back. The woman in the front passenger's seat turned around on her knees. "Hold her."

Hands gripped both of Adamescu's arms and the hair on her head. The woman leaned between the seats with a syringe in her hand. Adamescu squirmed backward, but the needle went into her neck.

She woke tied to a metal chair in a cellar built of mortared fieldstone. A piercing headache throbbed from behind her eyes. Her roller bag was open on the floor and her clothes were scattered.

"There you are." One of the women, petite, dark-complected, wearing a hospital gown over her clothes and throwaway latex gloves on her hands, stood in front of her. She spoke in English. "How about a drink of water?" She held a water bottle with a built-in straw to Adamescu's lips.

That's when Adamescu realized that she was naked. She tugged at her restraints. "Who took my clothes?"

"Cavity search. Go ahead, have a drink. Want me to drink first?"

Adamescu sucked on the straw. The water felt good going down. "Thank you."

"You bet."

"I'm cold. Can I have my clothes?"

"You know the drill. Less mess this way. And it makes it easier to get at the tender bits."

"I won't tell you anything."

"You don't have to convince me, honey. I'm just tasked with keeping you alive. Now the others, they're pissed. You messed up their normal routines, evaded capture for too long—they're going to come in hard. They want to know who you sold the nerve agent to."

"I don't know what you're talking about."

"It's been enough time that those people are already dead ends. Telling who they are won't make any difference."

"I've got nothing to say."

The woman called over her shoulder. "She's ready."

FOUR DAYS LATER, KD and Blunt were driving down a lane in the Italian countryside. Up ahead at the top of a ridge stood a small field-stone farmhouse. A Range Rover and a BMW were parked in the yard. As they approached, a woman wearing hiking clothes waved at them from the corner of the house.

Blunt glanced at KD. "You ever been to one of these before?"

"Interrogation?" She shook her head no.

"Think of the worst thing you could imagine."

"That bad?"

"Not always, but it's best to be prepared."

They parked next to the BMW. The woman was waiting at the door when they got out of their car.

"Stacy," Blunt said. "Who did you piss off to get assigned to this clusterfuck?"

"I could say the same for you."

"This is KD."

They shook hands.

The inside of the farmhouse was like the set of an old movie—potbellied stove, heavy wooden table, worn-out sofa. Two men sat at the table playing cards.

Blunt looked from Stacy to the men. "So she won't say anything?"

One of the men looked up from his cards. "Jen's keeping her alive for you."

Blunt turned to KD. "Let's get this over with."

They went down the rickety stairs into the cellar. The bulb shining down from overhead showed Adamescu, naked, tied to a chair. Her head hung down on her chest. Her body was covered in contusions. Some of her fingers were bent at odd angles. A line from a bag of saline hanging on a stand behind the chair snaked down into the crook of her arm. A dark-complected woman sat in the corner, reading a book.

"You must be Jen," Blunt said.

The woman nodded.

He looked back at Adamescu. "Christ, she's a mess. She hasn't told us anything?"

"Nothing of interest. Nothing actionable."

"This is horrible," KD said.

"I told you," Blunt replied.

She turned to Jen. "You're the medic?"

"Yep."

"Can't you help her?"

"Doc," Blunt said. "You know how this works. She can help herself. She starts talking, she gets the finest medical care available on the planet."

"This has gone too far."

"How many people have to die from the nerve agent before you think we haven't gone far enough?"

"We're better than this."

"Doc, we *are* this."

Blunt turned back to Jen. "When will she be able to talk and make sense?"

Jen looked at her watch. "She should regain consciousness any time now."

They went back upstairs. One of the men was gone and Stacy had taken his place.

"Want some coffee?" she asked.

"Where are the cups?" Blunt asked.

"In the cabinet next to the sink," she replied.

Blunt poured two cups of coffee and handed one to KD. "You got any sugar?"

Stacy shook her head no.

"What do you think about our guest?" the man asked.

"I think we're fucked," Blunt replied. "Don't see how we could do any better than you."

"So we can close this down?"

"Boss says we've got to talk to her once." He turned to KD. "Let's go for a walk."

Outside, the man who'd been playing cards was standing where Stacy had been standing when they drove up. "We'll keep watch for a bit," Blunt said.

The man went inside. Blunt and KD walked off across the short dry grass toward a large oak. They stood there for a few minutes sipping their coffee while they looked off down the hill into the valley they'd driven up through.

Finally, Blunt said. "So you don't think beating her some more will change her answers?"

"No. This is messed up, Blunt."

"It's turning into that situation where everyone starts pointing fingers, hoping the blame will stick to someone else. Who do you want to blame if it's not going to be her?"

"Are you serious?"

"We've been late all the way around on this job."

"We got the guns," KD replied.

"Sure. And we busted up one cell of the Fatherland Volk. But we're no closer to reacquiring the nerve agent than we were in the beginning. And we don't know what McCuller and Dayton were planning."

"Maybe Adamescu will respond to a little kindness."

"She's not talking. And Jacobs got shanked in jail. So we're probably never going to know."

KD's smartphone rang. It was Garcia. She put the phone on speaker.

"Are you at the farmhouse?"

"Yes."

"Have you spoken to the subject?"

"Not yet. She's supposed to regain consciousness pretty soon."

"But she still hasn't said anything?"

"Right."

"Leave her exactly as she is. Pull our people."

"Leave her?"

"A French extraction team is en route. They began tracking her in Spain but lost her in Barcelona."

"So they know who got the nerve agent?"

"She was going to sell it to one of their undercover operatives, but they missed their chance when the local police intervened. They want her and are willing to trade for something we want. It's a win-win."

"But the nerve agent is still out there."

"A politician in Rome was poisoned with a nerve agent the day before yesterday. Berlin station's team caught a break backtracking the surveillance cameras. Our team is setting up shop as we speak. I'm emailing you the info. Seize the nerve agent or destroy it."

KD and Blunt went back to the farmhouse. Stacy and the others were still sitting at the wooden table. "Grab your gear. We're all out of here."

"What about Adamescu?" Stacy asked.

"She's somebody else's problem. We need to be gone before they get here."

KD and Blunt waited until the others drove off. Then they went back downstairs and turned on the light. Adamescu's eyes were open. Blunt took a revolver from his coat pocket. "Last chance."

Adamescu smiled through bloody lips. "Let's get on with it."

"The French will be here in a little while."

"You're bluffing."

"You'll find out. Tell us who you sold the nerve agent to, and you come with us. Otherwise, you'll be shipped to a French prison hospital in Africa to be fattened up for round two."

She shook her head.

"Goodbye."

"Shoot me in the head before you go."

Blunt glanced at KD. "Waste of time."

They left the cellar light on, climbed the steps, and locked the door to the farmhouse on their way out.

"What was that about?" KD asked. "We already know where the nerve agent is."

"Maybe we do, maybe we don't. Couldn't hurt to get a little more information."

"But you were going to leave her no matter what she said."

"Boss said leave her, I leave her. Just thought we might catch a break if she was more afraid of the French than us."

They could hear helicopter blades chopping the air in the distance as they drove off the ridge and down into the valley. KD felt her phone vibrate. She'd received an encrypted email from Garcia. "We're taking the train to Rome."

11

KD and Blunt slept in their seats on the train on the trip south to Rome. At the Rome Termini train station, they fell in with the crowds hurrying off the train platforms and out to the huge main concourse. Rows of stores, like in any major airport, lined the interior. "There's the main entrance," Blunt said, pointing ahead of them.

"So that means we want the side entrance to our right."

They pulled their roller bags down the concourse and out onto the city street. The sidewalks were busy with pedestrians and the traffic was in knots, horns honking and brakes screeching. KD pointed at a BMW SUV in the loading zone. "There we are."

The driver, long hair down to his shoulders and tattoos on his arms, dark complexion of a southern Italian, got out of the SUV to shake hands. "I'm Lombardo." He spoke in a flat, Midwest American accent. "We got a couple hours of driving."

"Everything still quiet?" Blunt asked.

"No one knows we're here."

Lombardo pushed the SUV through the traffic, maneuvering through the other vehicles at every opportunity until they were out of the central city. "Everything going to plan?" KD asked.

"We're all set," Lombardo replied. "My boss will fill you in."

As they left the city, they got on the autostrade and drove off to the southwest into the wooded foothills of the Apennine mountains, where they got off on the regular highway and skirted a small town until they pulled up to a stucco single-story house on a deserted street. A bearded black man wearing casual clothes met them at the door. "Thompson," Blunt said, "it's been awhile. This is KD."

"Good to meet you," Thompson said. "Come on into the house."

The living room was empty except for two folding tables set against one wall. At one of the tables, a man wearing khakis, a golf shirt, and a soldier's haircut sat at a laptop computer. KD and Blunt followed Thompson through to the kitchen, where they sat at another folding table. "We've got a six-man team on loan," Thompson said. "You can check their credentials if you like."

"No need," KD said.

"The targets are in an abandoned factory about a mile from here. Paper trail indicates that the property is probably mob-owned. We've had it under surveillance since we got here yesterday. Their security is sloppy. Random patrols around the exterior. Everybody else up at the front of the building. There's been one visitor, a guy driving a van. His picture came up on the database as Free Italy Coalition."

"Rightwing anti-immigrant paramilitary?" Blunt asked.

He nodded.

"Where are the civilians?" KD asked.

"Factory went bankrupt in the financial crisis. Best intelligence is that the mafia has been using the area as a staging ground ever since. So there's nothing here now. Nearest population is about three miles east."

"What kind of surveillance have you got?" KD asked.

"Drone overhead. Five men on the perimeter. Just managed to place a snake camera through the wall this morning. Come on."

They went back into the living room to the man at the laptop. His screen showed a bird's-eye view of the factory. The place appeared to be abandoned. "Terry," Thompson said. "Give them a look-see through the snake."

Terry clicked on an icon at the corner of the screen. A video feed appeared. He clicked on the box in the corner to enlarge the image. Sheet plastic hung down from the ceiling, creating enclosed spaces within a larger room. People in full hazmat gear were working at lab equipment, but the camera was too far away for a detailed view.

"That doesn't look good," KD said. "Have we got the gear to go in?"

"The hazmat gear and extra equipment are due to arrive by morning," Thompson said. "Had to fly it in to keep the Italians out of the loop. In the meantime, we've rigged the building to collapse."

"Will the explosion burn hot enough to destroy the nerve agent?"

"I don't know. First priority is to contain the problem here. Nobody lives here. If a plume goes up, it won't spread far."

"If they're not manufacturing more nerve agent."

"What are you talking about, Doc?" Blunt asked.

"Do we know who those technicians are? Why they're suited up? What kind of equipment they have? Are they analyzing the nerve agent to make more? The amount in the canister—sure, probably not a big deal if it gets released on site. But what if there's more—a lot more?"

"How hard is it to manufacture?"

"I don't know. They used it kill a guy three days ago, so they had the canister open before that."

"We grabbed Adamescu four days ago," Blunt said. "We know she had the package five days ago. So that's the window for when she passed it along. That's all the time these people have had."

"Let's not get ahead of ourselves," Thompson replied. "The gear's going to come. We're going to go in hard, eliminate any opposition, grab the nerve agent. Case closed."

KD shook her head. "Can we wait until morning? We don't know their timeline. We need to know what they're doing in there."

"So we need to take a look," Blunt said. "It'll be dark soon. We'll reconnoiter. See what we can find out."

KD turned to Thompson. "Got any help for us?"

"I can spare two guys off the surveillance team."

KD and Blunt sat in the kitchen eating MREs while they studied the factory plans. The best spot to go in appeared to be an emergency exit located near the back of the building on the west side. "Think these plans are accurate?" KD asked.

Blunt shrugged. "Accurate from when they built the place. But now? We'll just have to keep our eyes open."

At nightfall, they went into a bedroom, stripped down to their underwear, and changed into black tactical gear and body armor. After they attached their night vision goggles to their helmets, Blunt tapped on his comms. "Check, check, check."

"Your comms are good," KD replied.

Blunt grinned. "You're looking like your old self, Doc."

"I can't lie," KD replied. "It does feel good to be geared up and out in the field."

Thompson was waiting for them in the living room. "You'll be using off-the-shelf Glocks and AR-15 rifles modified for auto fire. We don't want any shell casings that could be traced back to us. Lombardo will drive you in to where Miller and Chen are waiting. You ready?"

KD glanced at Blunt and nodded.

"Good luck."

Lombardo sat behind the wheel of a beat-up Fiat. KD and Blunt got into the back seat. KD turned on her comms set. "Check one, check two."

Terry replied from his laptop in the living room. "Loud and clear."

A few minutes later, Lombardo pulled over beside a half-collapsed garage next to the road. KD and Blunt slid out and scurried around to the back side of the garage. Miller and Chen, dressed in black tactical gear, were waiting. Even though a few clouds skittered across the sky, the moon provided plenty of light.

Miller and Chen led the way across a weedy field, past several large, rusty sheds, to the back of the factory. KD pointed to the left. They ran along the side of the building until they came to the emergency exit that KD had noted on the factory plans. There didn't appear to be any power in this end of the building. Miller jimmied the door with a pry bar. No alarm went off. KD pushed the door gently. A loud squeak reverberated into the dark interior. She stopped pushing when there was just enough room for them to slip through. They all dropped their night vision goggles into place. They were in a dusty room that was cut into cubicles. Some of the desks still had papers lying on them, although the computers and telephones were gone. All they could hear was their breathing.

Blunt took the lead. They moved at a crouch, examining the doorway for a laser alarm or tripwire before they moved into a long hall. KD whispered into her comms. "Straight ahead."

Light fell into the hall from the second room on to their right. As they approached, they heard voices carrying on a conversation in Italian. Blunt lifted his goggles and peeked around the corner. It was the cafeteria. Three men and two women, all wearing scrubs, were eating together at a round table. Another doorway at the end of the cafeteria led directly into another lit space.

Miller whispered into his comms. "Something about a deadline. Trouble with the aerosol. Need to alter the formulation? Want to get paid and go home. Can't quite hear everything."

Blunt whispered. "They're getting up."

KD, Blunt, Miller, and Chen waited for the techs to disappear into the next room before they scurried back the way they had come. As they were approaching the emergency exit, Terry's voice came over the comms. "Patrol moving toward you."

Blunt slung his rifle around to his back and pulled a knife from the sheath on his leg. He pressed his back against the wall beside the door. The others took cover on either side.

They heard voices. The door creaked all the way open. A man stepped in, his rifle at the ready. Blunt reached across, hugged the man to his side, and plunged his knife through the man's throat while KD reached in from the other side and pushed the barrel of the man's rifle up toward the ceiling. The man started to fall. KD snatched the rifle and pitched it behind her. The guy behind the first man opened fire. Blunt caught two rounds in his armor as he dropped to cover.

Miller and Chen fired through the doorway. Return fire stopped.

KD dove through the doorway, rolled twice, and shot the second man as he ran toward the front of the building. She spoke into her comms. "Fall back."

Blunt staggered out of the door, and then caught his balance. "You good?" she asked.

"I'm good."

Miller and Chen came out behind him. Men in street clothes, carrying automatic rifles, poured around from the front corner of the building and opened fire. KD, Blunt, Miller, and Chen ran back across the field, zigzagging from shed to shed, covering each other as they made their way back to the Fiat. Muzzle flash pulsed in the night, making it too hard to see if their shots were actually hitting anyone as they returned fire. When they got to the garage, Miller and Chen lobbed hand grenades back at their pursuers. Then they ran past the garage into the street. The Fiat was waiting. They all piled in. "Go! Go!" KD yelled.

Lombardo sped off, the car jostling along on the cracked asphalt. KD looked out the back window. Men were running into the street, firing at the Fiat just as it turned the first corner. Lombardo sped down the block, careened through a right turn, and regained control on the straightaway before he tapped the brakes and took a left. "We're in the clear," KD said.

When Lombardo pulled up in front of the safe house, KD, Blunt, Miller, and Chen piled out. Lombardo took off with the car.

Blunt turned to Miller and Chen. "Watch our perimeter."

KD and Blunt went into the house and dropped their gear by the door.

"What happened?" Thompson asked. "The drone can't see details in the dark."

KD filled him in.

"Anything broken?" Thompson asked Blunt.

"I'm breathing fine," Blunt replied.

"So it looks like the worst-case scenario," Thompson said. "Probable aerosolizing and manufacturing."

"Boss," Terry said, "Team One on comms."

Thompson put on his comms set. "Go." He listened for a minute. "Keep them under surveillance."

He turned back to KD and Blunt. "Twelve armed men total, two walking wounded. All headed back into the front of the factory. We can probably expect reinforcements."

"We can't let anyone leave there," KD replied.

"Maybe we should just collapse the building now," Blunt said.

"That will bring the fire department and the police," Thompson said. "If we involve the Italians, we'll have to tell them about the nerve agent. We can't do that."

"They're only twelve," KD said.

"That we know of," Thompson replied.

"We've got six, plus you and Lombardo, plus us," Blunt said. "Those are reasonable odds."

"Not including the technicians," Thompson said. "You saw five of them."

"They won't pose much of a threat in a gun fight."

"But what if they use the nerve agent against us?" Thompson asked.

"If they try to leave, that's a chance we'll have to take," KD replied. "First off, we need to take control of the access road into the factory. That's the only way in or out by vehicle. Lombardo's with us. We'll find a place to set up an ambush. Terry needs to stay here on surveillance and comms. At least for now. Miller and Chen can back up the other three guys if they're needed. You coordinate from here."

"Okay," Thompson said. "But let's try to avoid any contact until we have our hazmat suits."

KD, Blunt, and Lombardo, Lombardo behind the wheel, drove around the abandoned factory through a deserted neighborhood several blocks to the south, traveling on dark streets with their headlights turned off. KD looked at a GPS map on a small tablet computer. "Pull in here somewhere."

Lombardo turned in between two small houses and parked the Fiat.

They all got out. KD pointed to her left. "There's a railway over-pass over the access road into the factory due west. That's our spot."

They formed a loose V, Blunt in front and KD and Lombardo on his flanks, moving up the road at a slow trot, automatic rifles cradled in their arms, heads on the swivel for any motion in the dark, but all they saw were boarded-up windows, weeds, and trash. When they came to the railroad tracks, they turned and went up the tracks onto the overpass, where they reconned both sides before coming down to the access road on the side closest to the Fiat.

They crouched among the tall weeds and brush at the base of the overpass. Blunt was scanning the road leading away from the factory. "What are you thinking, Doc?"

"We need to cover the road in both directions. We're supposed to have our hazmat gear by morning. Until then, no one leaves. But rein-forcements? Right now, I say if they come, let them in."

"If there's only five or six, we could take them," Lombardo said.

"But keeping them pinned in the building will be easier than fighting out in the open. We won't be ready to breach the factory lab until we have our hazmat gear, so we want to contain the problem as long as possible."

Lombardo nodded.

KD continued. "I'll take the overpass. Lombardo, you take the road underneath. Blunt, you're in the ditch on the approach."

Blunt moved off down the side of the road at a crouch and slid down into the ditch about twenty yards back from the overpass. Lombardo made his way through the weeds to the concrete base of the overpass next to the road and squatted where he had a good line of sight in both directions. KD followed the railroad tracks up onto the overpass. She tapped her comms. "We're in place."

"Affirmative," Terry replied.

KD lay down on the gravel right of way where she had a clear view of the front of the factory. This was a straightforward little job. Hold the road. Take the factory in the morning. Get out before the Italians found out they were there. There was a simplicity to this work that she hadn't realized she'd missed. Of course, there was the danger, but that didn't seem important somehow. You live from when you're born until you die. It was the same for everyone. The only difference was how you lived. To know you were doing the right thing, that you were making a difference in your own small way, seemed incredibly important.

At 3:00 a.m., she heard Blunt's voice in her comms. "Light on the road."

She scrambled up onto her hands and knees to look over the tracks. A vehicle was coming down the road toward the factory. A huge vehicle, judging by the size and placement of the headlights. She lay down with her arms folded on the tracks to keep watch.

She heard Blunt's voice again. "I'm guessing armored car. Run-flat tires, bullet-proof glass." Jesus, she thought, if they loaded the nerve agent onto that vehicle, they'd have a hell of a time stopping them.

Lombardo's voice cut in. "What do you want to do, boss?"

"We can't let it in. Lombardo, with me now. Blunt, slow it down, but let it by."

KD waited for Lombardo to scramble up the bank. "We've not going to stop it by shooting at the sides. We need to take it from the roof."

As the armored car closed in, Blunt rushed up out of the ditch into the middle of the road, clicked his AR-15 to automatic fire, and sprayed the windshield of the oncoming vehicle. It seemed to slow a bit, but it didn't stop or give any indication that it would go around him. He stayed in the middle of the road, blasting away, switching out his empty magazine, the armored car's headlights bearing down on him, the windshield cracking into tiny fragments but not shattering. At the last moment, he dove out of the way, rolling across the pavement and down into the ditch, where he stood up to watch the van continue under the overpass.

KD was hanging from the back side of the overpass. Lombardo was standing above her, watching the armored car. As the hood of the van cleared the front of the overpass, he yelled. "Now."

KD dropped onto the roof of the armored car. She rolled off the side but managed to grab the cargo cage and scramble back up. The driver started weaving back and forth across the roadway. KD crawled up to the front of the armored car on the passenger's side, saw the door open, pulled her Glock, and waited for the man to reach up and grip the cargo cage before she fired. The man fell off the vehicle onto the road. KD grabbed the cargo cage with her free hand. The rear wheel bounced over the man. The door swung as the driver weaved back and forth, but the door didn't slam shut on its own. KD watched as another man's arm appeared, trying to grab the door handle as it swung in. KD holstered her gun, pulled a grenade from the cargo pocket of her pants, pulled the pin, and lobbed it into the armored car as the man was pulling on the door. Then she scrambled back a few feet and grabbed the cargo cage with both hands.

The explosion blew out the windshield. The headlights went out. The armored car slowed and veered off the roadway. As it started to fall onto its side into the ditch, KD sprang off and rolled across the turf. She scrambled to her feet. Lombardo and Blunt were running down the right of way toward her. She pulled her sidearm, went to the armored car where it lay on its side, and looked through the missing windshield. Two dead men were sprawled across the front seats. She turned toward the factory, but she couldn't see anything.

Lombardo and Blunt caught up to her. "You okay?" Blunt asked.

"I'm fine."

"Running and gunning, Doc. I knew you still had it in you."

KD smiled. "It was a close thing, but it worked out."

Lombardo peered toward the front of the factory. "The outside lights are on."

"Let's get back in place," KD said.

After they jogged back to the overpass, KD used her comms to contact Thompson. "Couldn't let them get that armored car in," she said.

"Everything's quiet at the factory," he replied.

"Hope it stays that way. How's our timeline?"

"Still solid."

. . .

Just before 5:00 a.m., KD, Blunt, and Lombardo made their way back to the safehouse. When they pulled up in front, they noted Miller and Chen in the shadows at opposite sides of the building, their rifles held across their chests. Inside, Terry was on the computer, monitoring the team at the factory, while Thompson was unpacking the hazmat suits.

"Finally," Blunt said. "Everything there?"

"Thus far," Thompson replied.

KD looked at the boxes stacked by the door. "What did we get for special explosives?"

"Thermite," Thompson said. "Have you ever worked with that stuff?"

"Took a class of exotic explosives. Thermite—burns at about 5000 degrees Fahrenheit, so it's about half as hot as the surface of the sun. Exactly what we need to snuff out the nerve agent." She pulled a box out of the stack and opened it on the folding table next to Terry. He scraped his chair back to give her more room. The bomb was a flat black rectangular box with a timer pad on the top. A remote detonator was taped to the side. "Blunt, have a look at this."

Blunt stepped over. "Complete setup. We can set a timer, use the remote, or override the timer with the remote. Belt and suspenders."

KD turned to Thompson. "What does surveillance show us?"

"Nothing is going on in the lab. We believe they're gathered near the front of the building."

"So they've closed shop and they're waiting for their ride." KD glanced at the others. "They aren't leaving with the nerve agent. Thompson, you're coordinating from here. Miller and Chen are with me and Blunt. We'll slip in the back, set the thermite. The other three guys, plus Lombardo, will hold the front of the factory. If we can take the nerve agent, great. Either way, that lab is done. We'll detonate the thermite, and you'll detonate the perimeter charges. If it all goes south, and you lose contact with us, blow the perimeter charges. That should set off the thermite. One way or another, we'll be done here by full light."

Lombardo dropped KD, Blunt, Miller, and Chen off on the back road next to the railroad tracks that ran down to the loading dock on the east side of the factory. They trotted along the tracks, Miller out front, KD and Chen on the wings, Blunt in the center carrying the thermite bomb in his backpack. Outside the loading dock, they slipped off their backpacks and pulled on the olive-colored hazmat suits over their tactical clothing. They put on the respirators and adjusted their hoods for a tight seal before they put on their night vision goggles. Then they put their backpacks back on and picked up their rifles.

KD spoke into her comms. "All good?"

"All good," Terry replied.

"Start the diversion."

Chen forced the security door next to the loading dock garage-style door. They stood there, waiting. When the heard gunfire from the front of the building, they went inside.

They moved through the building, watching for boobytraps at the doorways, KD guiding them from the building plans on a small tablet computer. The gunfire became louder and steadier as they moved along. Finally, they were in the lab. Equipment was still turned on and materials sat out in open containers as if the technicians had all rushed away in a hurry. Blunt opened the door on a lower cabinet, slipped his backpack off his shoulders, took out the thermite bomb, and set it on the shelf. KD squatted down beside him. "Set the timer for ninety minutes."

He tried to find her eyes through her mask. "Ninety minutes?"

"Ninety."

He set the timer on the bomb. KD set the timer on her watch for one hour and put the bomb remote detonator into the cargo pocket on her hazmat suit before she stood up and gestured to the others. They made their way back to the loading dock. She spoke into her comms. "We're out. How's the other team doing?"

"All under control."

They pulled off their hazmat gear and stowed it in their back-packs before they started to make their way back across the field. The first sign of dawn was glowing in the east. "Boss?" KD heard Lombardo in her comms.

"Go ahead."

"A vehicle's approaching."

"Like the other?"

"Not quite close enough to tell yet."

KD signaled for her team to stop. They hunkered down in the weeds. She got on her comms to Thompson.

"Definitely an armored car of some kind," he replied.

She paused for a moment. "Lombardo. Let it through."

KD turned to her team. "Another armored car. We don't have the firepower to stop it."

"So we can't let anyone get on it," Blunt replied.

"What are our orders?" Miller asked.

"Give me a minute." Blunt was right. If they loaded the nerve agent onto the armored car, there'd be no stopping them. The last time had been pure luck. And they'd been able to attack from the roof.

"Okay. We hit them from the inside. Try to force them back into the lab and away from the armored vehicle." She looked at the factory plans on her tablet. "See here?" They all leaned down over the tablet. "We go in where we went in the first time, but instead of stopping at the cafeteria, we move down adjacent to the lobby, fire into the lobby from these offices, try to push them back into the building."

"What about the armored car?" Chen asked.

"The other team will have to handle it."

"We've got sixty-eight minutes until the thermite blows," Blunt said.

"Then we better move," KD said.

She got on her comms. "Lombardo. We're coming up your left interior flank to drive the bad guys back into the building. Don't let anyone get out or get into the armored car."

"Affirmative."

KD and her team cut around the building to the emergency exit they had gone through before. It was hanging open just as they had left it.

They crept through the dark rooms, their night vision goggles on, moving as quickly as they could while staying on the lookout for an ambush. The occasional burst of gunfire reverberated from somewhere in front of them. When they slipped into the suite of offices next to the lobby, they could hear voices through the wall speaking in Italian. They moved silently toward the door to the lobby.

KD whispered into her comms. "Lombardo. We're in place."

Miller slipped a cable camera under the door, manipulating it to look around the room. The techs were huddled at the back of the lobby. The fighters were spread out across the front of the room, six large plastic cases in two stacks on the floor behind them. Whenever they tried to open the front door, a burst of gunfire penned them inside.

KD tapped her comms. "Lombardo. What do you see?"

"Armored car between us and the building. We've got them flanked. They can't get out of the building or the car."

"We're going in." She motioned to her team. "Suit up." They put on their hazmat suits and respirators.

Blunt cracked open the door to the lobby and rolled two flash-bang grenades into the room between the techs and the fighters and slammed the door. After the boom, he threw the door open and rolled into the smoke, Miller and Chen behind him, firing on the fighters, who were hollering and firing blind. A few seconds later, ten of the fighters were down. The last two put up their hands. Miller and Chen moved through the survivors, fighters and techs, zip-tying their wrists behind their backs.

KD's watch alarm buzzed. Blunt put his hand on her shoulder. "Thirty minutes," he said.

"I know." She tapped her comms. "We have control. Thermite in thirty minutes."

Miller and Chen herded the prisoners back through the offices toward the emergency exit.

KD and Blunt stood in the middle of the room, looking at the stacked cases. "What do you want to do about these?" Blunt asked.

"Can't get them past the armored car, too heavy to carry out the way we came, so they've got to stay. Let's move them closer to the thermite."

They each carried two cases back through the factory toward the lab. When they were in an outer room, Blunt said, "That's far enough, Doc. We're running out of time."

She nodded. They went back for the last two cases. "These are mine," Blunt said. "See you on the outside."

KD made her way back through the building. She got on her comms. "Lombardo. We're on our way out. What's happening?"

"Armored car is still in place."

"Fall back to the railroad overpass."

She caught up with Miller, Chen, and the prisoners in the field behind the factory. Several of the techs were straggling along as if they were still disoriented. "Keep moving," KD said. She pointed to the sheds by the road on the far side of the field. "There's going to be an explosion. We need to get to cover."

She looked at her watch. Ten minutes. "Come on. Hurry. Pick up the pace." Where was Blunt? She tapped her comms. "Blunt?"

"On my way."

She looked back toward the factory when they reached the first ramshackle shed. Blunt popped out of the emergency exit and began racing across the field. She looked at her watch. Five minutes.

She tapped her comms again. "Lombardo?"

"All behind the overpass. Armored car still in place."

"Four minutes," she said.

Blunt came around the corner of the shed and dropped to the ground. An explosion boomed from inside the factory. KD tapped her comms. "Thompson. Detonate the perimeter."

Four more explosions boomed in quick succession.

"Lombardo?"

"Factory demolished. Armored car got caught in the explosion. Isn't moving. Fire eating out from the center of the wreckage."

"Back to the safehouse."

KD turned to her team and the prisoners. "Get moving," KD said. They herded the prisoners toward the road. She tapped her comms. "Thompson, we've got seven to debrief."

"The nerve agent?"

"Lost in the fire."

"The chopper's almost here."

It was full morning by the time they were hustling down the deserted street to the safehouse. A helicopter, the rotors turning, sat in the street. Thompson and Terry were loading cases of equipment onboard. Three men in black tactical gear moved the prisoners onto the helicopter.

KD turned to Blunt. "What took you so long?"

"Moved the cases back to the lab."

"That was a crazy thing to do. They were close enough."

"Sometimes close enough ain't good enough."

A BMW SUV careened into the yard. Lombardo and the other soldiers got out. Thompson waved them toward the chopper, but Lombardo joined Thompson as he walked across the yard toward KD and Blunt.

"Good day's work," Thompson said. "I'll take your gear. The house is empty except for your civilian clothes and bags. Lombardo will take you where you need to go. Better get a move on. We've got ten minutes left on the fire truck response time."

KD and Blunt went into the little house. KD wanted a shower, just to wash the evidence off her body, but she knew that would have to wait. They stripped off their tactical gear in the bedroom, pulled on the clothes they'd been wearing before, opened the envelopes that contained their new IDs, credit cards, and smartphones, rinsed their faces in the kitchen sink, and bundled their military gear into their backpacks. They did a walk-through. The house was empty.

When they came outside, Miller ran across the yard and took the backpacks.

Lombardo was waiting in the BMW. Blunt got in the front and KD got in the back. She felt her phone vibrate. She had a message. *Private airstrip south of Rome.*

She tapped Lombardo on the shoulder. "You know an airstrip south of Rome?"

"I know the one."

The helicopter took off, flying low to the west. Lombardo put the SUV in gear. "All those people are going to wish they were in some other line of work."

"At least they're still alive," Blunt said.

"If you call that living."

Lombardo turned down a side road, working his way down the narrow lanes that cut between the pastures and farm fields, taking the SUV well away from the factory fire before he came out on the main highway. KD lay across the back seat. So this was what success looked like. They'd disrupted a Fatherland Volk cell, interfered with a plot by the Peoples Freedom Party, and destroyed the nerve agent. Not too many dead. Not good guys anyway. And the whole thing started because some pharma execs wanted to make some money—if Rawlings was to be believed. Crazy times. Crazy, crazy times.

When she woke, they were pulling through the chain-link gate at the airstrip. A small jet sat on the tarmac one hundred yards away from the building that housed the business office. Two planes were parked in front of open hangars. A man in blue coveralls waved them toward the jet. Lombardo pulled up near the stairs into the plane.

KD and Blunt got out of the BMW with their bags. "You staying?" KD asked.

"I've got a few things to clear up," Lombardo replied. "This is my turf."

"Thanks for the ride," Blunt said.

"I'll see you when I see you." Lombardo circled around the jet and drove back toward the gate.

KD and Blunt looked up at the empty doorway to the jet. "No crew," Blunt said.

"Maybe we don't rate first-class treatment," KD replied.

"Maybe. You got your personal weapon?"

"Ankle holster. You think this is a trap?"

"I'm not thinking. I'm running on adrenaline and intuition. Never go in a place you can't get out of. Can you fly a plane?

"I'm not rated for this."

A man wearing a pilot's uniform appeared in the doorway. Blunt put his hand on the pistol in his jacket pocket. "Sorry for the delay," the pilot said. "Had orders to wait until your friend was gone. Welcome aboard."

Blunt took his hand out of his pocket. "Where are we going?"

"I don't know your final destination. I'm flying you into Ramstein."

Blunt turned to KD. "Guess we're catching a ride home with the air force. Know anyone there?"

"Not in a long time."

They climbed up the stairs into the airplane, passed through the galley into the passenger compartment, and set their bags on the nearest seats.

"We'll be at Ramstein in an hour and a half," the pilot said. "There's a shower in the bathroom. Help yourself to the food in the galley. Anything you leave on the plane will be taken care of."

12

Twenty-four hours later, they were driving away from Joint Base Andrews, Maryland, in a car from the National Defense Agency motor pool, heading northwest to their headquarters in Suitland, Blunt behind the wheel.

"I'm going to be glad to be sleeping at home tonight," Blunt said.

"Does your wife know you're back?"

"I'll call her from the landline at the office." A SUV cut into their lane. Blunt pressed his brakes and tapped his horn. "DC drivers. Most of them can only see in front of themselves." He put on his turn signal and changed lanes. "What about you, Doc? Happy to be home?"

"I don't know if happy is the right word. My life's not as simple as yours. You've got your wife and your kids. I've got an empty apartment and a lot of bad memories."

They drove along in silence for a few minutes.

"So what do you think of the job, Doc?"

"Is this a normal assignment?"

"Is anything really normal?"

"I need a better apartment and someone I can count on."

Blunt smiled. "You can count on me, Doc."

"You know what I mean."

"I know what you mean."

"So this job's all done."

Blunt laughed. "Wish it was. We've still got to face the paper-work." Blunt glanced at her. "So come on, Doc. What do you really think? Enough excitement? Making enough difference? Think you'll stick it out?"

"It's the only thing in my life that completely makes sense, Blunt, so I guess I'm going to do it until something better comes along."

MAJOR HOWARD RAWLINGS, sportscoat and khakis, sat in a booth at a hotel bar. A middle-age white man and a slightly younger black woman, nondescript suits and expressionless faces, sat across from him, Mr. Smith and Ms. Jones. He'd worked for them before, promised himself he'd never work for them again, but these were lean times for a crew like his. The kind of job he wanted was a straight-up package retrieval—air support, safehouses, full expense account, and diplomatic immunity if it all turned to mud. The kind of job that Smith and Jones offered generally included iffy intelligence, paying expenses out of your pocket, and complete disavowal if the job went sideways. But a man's got to eat.

"So you're telling me there's a guy in a friendly country who you want picked up, and you don't want the friendlies to know we did it. If fact, you don't want them to know that the guy is even gone."

"Nobody's watching him," Ms. Jones said. "The only people who want him are us."

"And this job has been sanctioned?"

"That's a strong word," Mr. Smith said. "Let's just say that your Uncle Sam wants this job done, and he doesn't want anyone to know about it. Not the friendlies, not the CIA, not any federal law enforcement."

"This guy is unprotected?"

"He better have protection, the kind of women he's been running with, but, yeah, no bodyguards of any kind."

"What's the exfil?"

"You get our guy across the border; there'll be a plane waiting."

"We're talking European Union?"

"Yes."

"One guy on his own, out in the open, suspecting nothing?"

"Yes."

"A guy nobody else wants?"

"That's right."

"I can do it for thirty thousand."

"Why don't you and your guys fly coach?" Ms. Jones asked.

"Twenty thousand should get the job done," Mr. Smith said. "It's just a simple grab."

"You supplying the weapons? Twenty-eight. It's as low as I can go."

"Twenty-three plus the gear, all NATO stock."

"Twenty-five and we keep the gear."

"You drive a hard bargain."

"Then we're on."

"This guy has to be alive when you deliver him," Ms. Jones said.

"Of course."

Mr. Smith handed him a thumb drive. "All the details are there. I'll text the pickup location for the gear. We need this done immediately."

"If it's like you say, you'll have your guy within the week." Rawlings slid out the booth and walked out of the bar.

"Did you get all that, Ms. Han?" Ms. Jones spoke into the microphone under her shirt.

"Yes," Tina replied, "the mics worked perfectly."

"So we're off the hook?"

"I just handle the tech. You'll need to talk to the boss about your arrangement. Give Rawlings a few more minutes and then bring me my gear."

TINA WAS SITTING in the back of an electrician's van across the street from the hotel. She took off her comms set and took out her phone.

"Rawlings took the job, boss. Smith and Jones wanted to know if you're finished with them."

"Tell them I'll be in touch. That should make them squirm."

GARCIA ROLLED BACK her office chair and put a single sheet of paper into her shredder. The Poles would arrest Rawlings and his crew as soon as they tried for their target. If they managed to escape and make it back to the US, the FBI would scoop them up and hold them for extradition. Accelerated Results Associates would be off the board permanently. After Rawlings and his team were safely locked away, a message would go out through back channels to all the contractor outfits explaining the real reason for their imprisonment. No one breaks into US government facilities without paying the price.

LATER THAT WEEK, KD met Frank for dinner at a white cloth Italian restaurant. She was wearing a dress with a white sportscoat. Frank was still wearing the suit he'd worn to his meetings that day. The check was lying on the table between them. "So that's what's been going on since I saw you last," KD said.

"All of it?"

"Most of it. Some of the details are classified." She sipped her sparkling water. She'd barely touched her glass of red wine. "I've still got a few faded bruises. Didn't want to have to explain them later."

Frank smiled. "So, are you going to show me your apartment?"

"No, not yet."

"Why not?"

"We're not playing house. We're not just falling back into the way things were. You broke my heart, and I'm not over that yet. Not completely. Even if we're talking and sleeping together. So if you want to be with me, we're going to your hotel."

"And if I say no?"

"Then I know where you stand. We can say goodbye. You can be with me on my terms, or not at all."

"How long have you been thinking about this?"

"It's been burbling up."

"What about the future?"

"I don't know. Things will stay the same or they'll change. But if they change, it's going to mean something."

"Don't I get a say?"

"You had a say, and you chose to piss it away for a fantasy that wasn't going to come true. Chose a faceless woman and a faceless baby over me. I'm sorry, but that's how I see it when the anger wells up. So now it's my way until I really believe I can trust you."

"Katie, you can trust me. You're the only woman I care about. I was so, so stupid, but I know better now."

She shrugged. "You don't get to decide if I can trust you. All you get to decide is if we're going to keep seeing each other. Do you want to keep doing this?"

"Yes, I do. I've got to keep hoping I can make this thing right."

"Then ask me up to your room."

A NOTE FROM THE AUTHOR

Thanks for reading *The Hunt for the Hijacked Nerve Agent*. If you enjoyed it, please post a short review on a review site of your choice. A few words will do. Honest reviews are the number one way I attract new readers.

Thanks so much.

I'd love to hear from you. You can reach me at my website: https://michaelpking.org

ALSO BY MICHAEL P. KING

The KD Thorne Thrillers

The Hunt for the Hijacked Nerve Agent

Murder at Mercy Creek

The Travelers

The Double Cross: A Travelers Prequel

The Traveling Man: Book One

The Computer Heist: Book Two

The Blackmail Photos: Book Three

The Freeport Robbery: Book Four

The Kidnap Victim: Book Five

The Murder Run: Book Six

The Casino Switcheroo: Book Seven

Thicker Than Thieves: Book Eight

The Dark Web Scam: Book Nine